My life behind the scenes at...

Heart Magazine

Search for a star

Cindy Jefferies

USBORNE

For sailor Paul, with love

First published in 2011 by Usborne Publishing Ltd., Usborne House,
83-85 Saffron Hill, London EC1N 8RT, England.
www.usborne.com

A CIP catalogue record for this book is available from the British Library.

JFMAMJJ SOND/11 02347/1 ISBN 9781409520221
Printed in Reading, Berkshire, UK.

Holiday jobs

It was the beginning of the summer holidays, and Ellie Ixos had six weeks stretching ahead of her. Some of her friends were looking forward to a lazy summer, with a bit of swimming, lots of parties and hopefully, if the weather was good enough, plenty of barbecues. Others, like her best friend Hannah, were planning on earning some money. Hannah was off to Spain with her mum, dad and older sister in a couple of weeks, and was determined to earn some extra cash by working in her aunt's shop before she went. She already had a list of things she wanted to bring back.

"Clothes are fantastic out there," she told

Ellie. "I need some new sandals, but I'm going to wait until I get there before I buy any. And last year I saw a brilliant leather jacket, but I'd spent all my holiday money, and couldn't afford it. This year I'm going to make sure I earn enough to buy one." She looked suddenly stricken. "I hope I like this year's designs!"

Ellie laughed. "They'll have something you'll love, I'm sure." She paused, thinking of Hannah enjoying her holiday, while she would be spending the summer at home in London. "I'll miss you when you go," she said.

Hannah, who was lying on the grass in her back garden, sat up. "No you won't. You'll be too busy being a cool journalist at *Heart* magazine. With all the excitement of that you'll never miss me."

Ellie gave her a teasing grin. "That's true." There certainly were compensations for Ellie in spending the summer holidays at home, and she couldn't wait to get back to work at the magazine. It really was a job to die for.

Hannah pouted and poked her friend in the ribs. "Well!" Then she relented. "And that's fine. I don't mind. After all, I'm going to be having fun. And you'll need something to do to keep you out of trouble while I'm away."

Ellie rolled over onto her stomach and picked a long strand of grass that the mower had missed. "Tomorrow," she said, absently chewing the stalk, "you'll be stacking shelves, and I'll be fetching the *Heart* editor's coffee order. What glamorous lives we lead!"

Hannah poked her friend again. "You wait. By the time I get back from Spain you'll probably have appeared on TV, been invited onto some megastar's yacht, and interviewed all the most famous actors and musicians in the world!"

Ellie giggled. "Don't exaggerate!"

All the same, it *was* exciting to be going back to work at *Heart*. So far, Ellie had interviewed Pop and Lolly Lowther, the famous modelling pop stars, and had found herself on a photo shoot with Zone One, her absolute favourite boy band. She still felt a pang when she remembered how Al had looked deep into her eyes as he had sung to her. Her secret dream was that she would meet him again, and he would ask her out. She knew it would never happen, but all the same...

Reluctantly, she turned over and stood up. The shadows were lengthening, and it was time she went home. She gave her best friend a hug. "Good luck tomorrow."

Hannah hugged her back. "And you."

"See you online?"

"Of course."

"Bye then!"

"Bye!"

Now it was the following morning, and Ellie was at the stunning office building in the city, where *Heart* had its home. On the way up in the lift she double-checked that she had the old notebook she always carried. It had belonged to her father, and she liked to think it brought her luck. It also connected her to him in a very special way, because he'd died before she'd been born. All through the notebook were helpful phrases he had written out for himself. The first, and the one that she liked best so far was *You can do this!*

Ellie got out of the lift on the third floor and when she reached the lobby she changed into the shoes she'd brought with her to wear in the office. The Editor in Chief, Angel Makepiece, was *very* fussy about her white carpet, and about her staff too. Before going into the large, open-plan office, Ellie checked her hair and make-up. It would never do to look anything but as perfect as she could manage.

There was a new girl at the reception desk. She looked a few years older than Ellie, with long dark hair and beautiful, slanted black eyes.

She looked at Ellie and smiled.

"Welcome to *Heart, the magazine to die for*," she said. "Can I help you?"

"I'm Ellie Ixos," said Ellie, showing her ID. "I've come to work for the summer."

"Of course – Ellie!" the girl seemed delighted to meet her. "I'm Debbie Wu. I've heard all about you from Piano."

"Really?" Ellie was sure that if Piano, or Pea-Are-No as she liked her name to be pronounced, had talked about her to Debbie, the conversation wouldn't have been very positive. Piano had always resented Ellie, right from the first day, when she had arrived for the work placement arranged by her Uncle Patrick, who was on the board of *Heart* magazine.

Debbie Wu glanced behind her, and then gave Ellie a knowing smile. "It's all right," she said. "I've heard a bit from Francesca too. I listen to both sides, and can make up my own mind about people."

Ellie shrugged. She hoped that was true. And maybe Piano had decided that, if Ellie was going to keep working at *Heart*, it would be worth her while being a bit nicer to her. If so, it would be a great relief to Ellie.

"Do you know if I have my own desk?" she asked. "Last time I used Piano's, but that was because she was on reception."

"I'm pleased to say that you do!" Debbie looked almost as happy as Ellie felt. "Or at least, Angel and Francesca decided it would be a good idea to have a spare for freelancers, and while you're here, that means you. We've had a bit of a rethink in the office," she went on. "And they delivered the desk last week. It's over by the window."

Ellie looked, and realized that there had indeed been a few changes. The water cooler had gone, and in its place there was a new desk. It was right beside the window, so she'd have a wonderful view.

"Fantastic! Where is everyone though?"

"Piano and Francesca are having an editorial meeting with Angel in her office," said Debbie. "I think they're trying to look at their work deadlines to see what they can do to make it a bit less of a scramble to get each issue out."

"Deadlines can be pretty stressful," agreed Ellie, remembering how tough it had been meeting Angel's deadline for her article about Zone One. Her day with the band had been brilliant, but writing it up under pressure hadn't been quite so much fun.

She went through the reception area, and over to have a look at her new workplace. The desk was blonde wood, with space underneath to store her laptop, and there were two little drawers to one side. There was a comfortable-looking chair, and when she gazed through the window she had a view of the office building opposite, and the street below. For a moment she stared down at the traffic. She could hear hardly any street sounds from here, three floors up.

She sat down, opened her *Heart* laptop and switched it on. Her email inbox contained a short, friendly welcome message from Francesca, the Deputy Editor, a similar one from Angel, that was so impersonal it had to have been used for every employee since Angel had become Editor, and another email entitled *Brief,* that also came from Francesca's address. There wasn't a welcome message from Piano, but then, Ellie hadn't really expected one.

It was wonderful that Angel Makepiece had decided they needed someone of the magazine's target age in the office, and even more wonderful that she'd asked Ellie to be that person. That, and the fact that she got on well with Francesca, more than made up for Piano not liking her. She clicked on *Brief* and it opened.

Your brief this summer is to list people that you think Heart readers would like to see featured, then contact and interview them! We already have an in-house list, but hope you might be able to add to it. Email me some names for us to discuss. Then we can decide who you should contact first. Make absolutely no approaches until after I've given you the go-ahead.

Ellie leaned back in her seat, her heart suddenly beating very hard. What a fantastic brief! She could think of dozens of people she'd love to read about...and meeting them would be even better. She didn't feel even the tiniest bit envious of Hannah and her Spanish holiday now. This was going to be the summer of a lifetime!

Her fingers flew over the keyboard as she scrambled to put down all her favourite band members, singers and film stars. She wondered if she really would get to meet some of them over the next six weeks. She knew that it could take a while to set up interviews, so there was no time to lose.

After half an hour she had a long list, and she spent the next few minutes arranging it so that her very favourite people were at the top. She knew she wouldn't have time to get through anything like all of them, so she might as well put the ones she liked best, first. As soon as she'd finished, she emailed the list to Francesca, feeling very pleased with herself. She looked at her watch and saw that there was time to spare before she needed to fetch the staff their coffee. She reckoned she'd done *really* well with her first job.

"Ellie?" It was Francesca, back from her meeting with Angel, and she was smiling.

"Hi!" said Ellie, beaming at the Deputy Editor. "It's great to be back."

"It's good to have you back," said Francesca, looking at her laptop screen. "And I see you've lost no time in getting a list of people back to me."

"Well, I thought I ought to get on with it," said Ellie, feeling pleased.

Francesca picked up a sheet of paper from her desk and offered it to Ellie. "This is our in-house list," she said. "It looks as if most of the people you mention are already on it. But there are a couple we hadn't thought of." She glanced at her screen again, and then back to Ellie. "Charlie Daniels...his name rings a bell but I can't place him...who is he?"

"He wrote the wonderful fantasy trilogy, *Fanghurst*," said Ellie. "The books that are being made into three films. The first film was *amazing*! I went to see it with my friend Hannah. I'm not surprised it won so many awards. And the second one is coming out soon. I can't wait!"

"Oh, of course!" Francesca looked annoyed with herself. "Yes, I should have known. I'm sure Joe will take some pictures of the actors arriving on the red carpet when it opens. But I haven't seen anything about the author. Has he written anything else?"

"I don't think so," said Ellie. "I can check, but I think they might have been his first books."

"Well," said Francesca, looking thoughtful, "we don't usually interview authors, but this certainly was a huge film deal. There might be a good story in it. Why don't you have a bit of a dig around online and see what you can find out about Charlie Daniels? Maybe he should go to the top of our list. He'd be someone a bit different for a change, and we might be able to tie an interview in with the new film when it comes out."

"Okay," said Ellie. She glanced at the in-house list and noticed another omission. "What about Zone One?" she said, thinking about the boys in her favourite band – especially Al.

Francesca laughed. "You can't keep interviewing the same boys," she said. "Just because you like them."

Ellie blushed.

"Go on. Have a look for Charlie Daniels. We can decide if you ought to try and get an interview when we know a bit more about him. Okay?"

"Okay," said Ellie. She studied the list more carefully and felt surprised. "There are quite a few people on here that *I* don't know," she said to Francesca.

"That's probably because they're up and coming." Francesca gave Ellie a teasing look. "Some of the musicians are working on albums that will be really big in a year or so's time."

"Wow," said Ellie, impressed. "Well, I'll get searching for Charlie Daniels."

Ellie did intend to search for him, but she couldn't resist keying in one or two of the names on the in-house list that she hadn't recognized. One was an actor who had only had a couple of small parts in TV dramas, but who looked absolutely gorgeous. Another was a singer in a band she'd never heard of. The band had some music online, and Ellie made a note to listen to it when she was at home. Then she got down to the job in hand.

Authors didn't often become well known, and Ellie couldn't think of anything at all that she'd read about Charlie Daniels, although she'd loved his books. She didn't know if he was young or old, or whether he lived in England or not. But when she googled his name she discovered that he had a website and a blog, so it was going to be easy enough to find out about him.

Ellie spent some time reading his website, his blog and anything else she could find that mentioned his name. Eventually she sat back in her chair and rubbed her eyes.

"Francesca?"

"Yes? How are you doing?"

Ellie bit her lip. "Charlie Daniels is odd. I can't quite work it out."

"What's the problem? Isn't he very interesting?"

"No, it's not that." Ellie twisted in her seat so she could look at Francesca properly. "I think our readers would love to know more about him. But in spite of reading loads about his *books* I can't find out anything about what he looks like, how old he is, where he went to school...there's nothing!"

Sophie has some news

Francesca stared at Ellie. "Really? Doesn't he have a website?"

"Ye-es," said Ellie. "But there's not much on it."

A slight smile touched the corners of Francesca's mouth. "That's why you do research, Ellie. I thought you knew that. Not everyone puts their whole life history on their websites. How about Facebook?"

"Tried that," said Ellie. "I *have* been doing research. I've googled him, read his website and blog from beginning to end, and anything else I could find, but it's all so insubstantial."

"Well that might actually make him more

interesting," said Francesca, smiling properly now. "Perhaps he's a bit shy. Some authors are, I believe. But there must be some contact details somewhere. Maybe you'll get a scoop. I don't recall seeing him interviewed anywhere else. Go for it! But before you do, you might as well fetch our coffee. It'll soon be time, and no doubt Angel will be asking where hers is in a moment."

Ellie closed the lid of her laptop and sighed. Francesca expected initiative, and usually Ellie had plenty of that, but at the moment, with this project, she was feeling a bit frustrated. She was sure that if *she* had a website, and she'd written a fantastic series of books, she'd *definitely* be blowing her own trumpet, and including lots of pictures of herself with the stars of the film. True, on the website there were some photos of the actors, but not one of Charlie Daniels himself, not even a single publicity photo, and yet she knew that most authors had at least one of those. On the other hand, Francesca was right. It made him rather mysterious, and it would be fun if she could track him down. She just needed to work at it a bit, and use her imagination.

She paused at reception on her way out to fetch the coffee. "How do you like your coffee, Debbie?" she asked. "I'm just off to get some for everyone."

"I don't drink coffee," Debbie told her. "I like Earl Grey tea best." She smiled at Ellie. "I make myself a drink in the kitchen whenever I want one."

"Oh." The small kitchen off the lobby was hardly used by anyone else. Ellie wondered what Piano made of that. She could imagine her sneering at the very idea of tea.

Ellie warmed to Debbie. Anyone who seemed comfortable to be a bit different was okay by her. "See you in a while then," she said. She hurried to the lift, and when it came she took it down to the basement.

Ellie should simply have gone to the ground floor, and out at the front of the building, but she had a few minutes to spare, and she wanted to go and say a quick hello to Sophie, her best friend in the building. Sophie was the post girl, and was kept busy servicing all the offices. Her boyfriend Flynn also worked in the building. He was part of the IT Department that existed to keep all the computers up and running. He was very good-looking, and was Ellie's second favourite person working at Heart.

As soon as Sophie saw Ellie she dropped what she was doing and gave her a big hug. "How *are* you?" she cried. "I was hoping I'd see you. I thought it was today, and then I wasn't so sure. I wondered if I'd got the date wrong. So how's life treating you?"

"Fine," said Ellie, hugging Sophie back. Although Ellie only saw her when she was at work, Sophie felt like the big sister Ellie had never had. "Been busy though." She explained about her brief and Sophie looked impressed.

"Sounds great," she said with enthusiasm. "It's good they've given you a longer-term project this time, as you'll be here for a while over the summer."

"I'm having difficulty with the person they want me to tackle first though," said Ellie. "And it's really frustrating because I actually suggested him! I don't have time to chat for too long now because I have to fetch the coffee, but it's Charlie Daniels, and I can't even find out what he looks like. None of the information on his website gives any clues."

"Have you tried his publisher?" asked Sophie. "I bet they have loads of stuff they could email you."

Ellie stared at her. "Sophie, you're a genius. Why on earth didn't I think of that? I could use them to get in touch with him for an interview too!"

Sophie laughed. "Probably. But I'm not a genius. On the other hand..." She beamed from ear to ear. "I think I may have sold a pot."

Ellie's eyes widened in excitement. Sophie was a struggling studio potter. As well as working in the post room, she had been trying for some time to get her work noticed by collectors. "Really?" said Ellie. "That's amazing news. Well done!"

Sophie bit her lip. "Don't get too excited. It's not totally certain yet, but I'm hopeful. Anyway, you must go. You don't want Angel on the warpath."

"True," said Ellie, "I'll come and have lunch with you if that's okay. You can tell me all about it then."

"Okay. See you later."

Ellie made her way back upstairs and out onto the street. Coffee! Coffee! where she had to collect the coffees was only a few metres away. Luckily there wasn't much of a queue, so

Ellie was able to get back to the office in good time. She handed Francesca her drink, and went to put one on Piano's desk.

"What's that?" said Piano, pointing one emerald green, painted nail at the carton.

Ellie looked at it with puzzlement. "What do you mean? It's your coffee of course."

Piano sighed theatrically. "And no doubt it's full of dairy produce."

For a moment Ellie wasn't sure what Piano meant. Then she realized. "Milk, yes. It's a skinny latte, like you always have."

Piano sighed again, and shook her head. "I haven't had a latte for *ages*. Not in the morning, anyway." She counted off her requirements on her fingers. "In the morning I have a double espresso, and in the afternoon I have a single espresso, followed by a skinny latte at three o'clock."

Ellie glared at her. "You could have told me. Or you could have emailed me what you wanted if you didn't actually choose to speak to me. I'm not psychic you know! But, as you *didn't* do that you have a skinny latte, with lots of dairy produce. Tough luck!" She stomped off to Angel's office feeling thoroughly annoyed with herself for letting Piano get to her. Every time, she planned to rise above it, and every time Piano somehow got under her skin.

She knocked at Angel's door and sidled in, carefully carrying the coffee upright. It had a lid on it so it shouldn't spill, but she really didn't want Angel snapping at her after her run-in with Piano.

Angel looked up from her desk and appraised Ellie for a few moments without speaking. It was totally unnerving when the Editor did this. Ellie was always worried that her make-up might be smudged, or her clothes unacceptably creased, but so far she hadn't been told off for any mistake in the unofficial and unspoken *Heart* office dress code.

Angel motioned for Ellie to put the coffee on her desk and turned her gaze back to the two handbags in front of her. One was a classic shape in black, with a gold clasp, while the other was a strikingly boxy design in brick-red leather. There were more bags on the glass table by the long white sofa. It looked like *Heart* would soon be doing a feature on bags. Ellie wanted to say that she loved the red one, but wasn't confident that her opinion would be gratefully received. Instead, she turned to go.

"Thanks, Ellie. It's nice to have you back."

Ellie turned and said, "Thank you!" But Angel was contemplating the bags again, and it was as if she had never spoken. Even so, she must be in favour if Angel thought it was nice to have her back! Now, all she had to do was track down Charlie Daniels, and conduct a brilliant interview. Then she'd *really* be flavour of the month.

3
A question of pots

Ellie had a quick look on her laptop at the file of articles planned for next month's issue of the magazine so far. As she had suspected, the main fashion feature was to be on bags of all sorts and sizes. There was also an article on a film star. She skimmed it, and wondered who had written it. It wasn't an interview, the film star was American, and hadn't been in England for ages. The article hadn't been the result of a phone call either, which was sometimes the way *Heart* journalists spoke to celebrities. Ellie decided that it must have been put together using websites and blogs. She hoped she wouldn't have to do that with Charlie Daniels.

If she did, it would be a very thin article indeed, and hardly worth printing. But then, if *she* was having problems finding out much about him, other journalists must be as well. She put her chin in her hands and leaned on her desk. Maybe there wasn't much written about him because it was just too much bother for most journalists to winkle out the facts, but...*she* had the time to have a go.

Ellie's heart started to tick a little harder. If only she *could* get hold of Charlie Daniels. With the films being such a huge hit lots of magazines might suddenly decide he was a hot topic. How cool would it be if she was the first to write an article about him? There was plenty from the newspapers after the opening of the first film in the trilogy. Some people claimed that he had attended the premiere, but with no pictures to prove it, maybe he hadn't. Ellie decided to check his website again, to make sure that she hadn't missed anything, and then to try his publisher, as Sophie had suggested. She could also try emailing his agent, if she could track down who it was. Surely he must have one? Ellie Ixos thought of her father's phrase *You can do this!* Like him, she didn't intend to give up easily.

Ellie trawled through the website again, and found absolutely no way of contacting him direct. Lots of authors had a "contact me" bit on their websites. Ellie had used them herself occasionally, when she had read and enjoyed a particular book and wanted to tell the author how much she'd loved it. Surprisingly often the authors would reply, but she guessed that Charlie Daniels wasn't the sort of author who thought it important to keep in touch with his readers.

She went to the publisher's website, and onto a page that was devoted to the Fanghurst Trilogy. There was a competition to win a beautiful silver chain, which, in the book, was worn by a particularly scary time-travelling character. It would make a lovely necklace for any normal human being. Ellie was pleased she'd looked at the site. *I'll go in for the competition,* she thought. *I might even win! But I'll have to wait until I get home. There are a couple of really difficult questions and I need to find the answers in the first book...if only I can find the reference without having to read the whole story again.*

She didn't actually consider that too much of a hardship. It would be fun reading the book again. But then, all at once, Ellie felt as if she was being deflected from her real purpose, to interview the author himself. The whole website page had been designed to sell books, without giving away any snippets of author information. Once again, there was no way of contacting the author, but there was a general phone number and email address for the publisher. She wondered about phoning, but felt a bit shy. In the end, without a lot of hope she sent a brief message, saying who she was, which magazine she worked for, and how much she would love to interview Charlie Daniels. She made a lot of the fact that she was a very young, wannabe journalist, who totally loved his books – just in case that helped. Then, after a lot of effort, trawling through a load of online newspaper articles that referred to him in some way, she finally managed to find out which literary agency Charlie Daniels was with. It was a big firm, with lots of agents, and it took a while to track down which one was his. Once again she sent an email, and hoped for the best.

Ellie sat back in her chair and let out a sigh. She hadn't realized how hard she'd been concentrating. She felt as if she'd been staring at the screen for days.

"You haven't gone for any lunch yet, have you, Ellie?" said Francesca. "Why don't you go now? You look as if you need to get away from that screen for a while."

"Okay, thanks," said Ellie. "I think I will."

Francesca was right. Ellie did need a break. She grabbed her bag and went down to see Sophie, as she had promised.

"I thought you weren't coming!" said Sophie as soon as she appeared. "Flynn's been and gone again, but he said he'd try to drop by for a coffee later. There was a networking problem up in the Art Department, but it shouldn't take long."

Ellie pulled out a stool and sat at the old, wooden table that Sophie used to sort mail on. Sophie had been franking some mail to go out, but it was pushed to one side at the moment.

"So tell me all your news," Ellie called to Sophie, who had gone into the back room to put the kettle on. "What's this about the pot?"

"Well!" Sophie reappeared with a smile on

her face. "Like I said, it's not confirmed yet, but a man phoned me up the other day and said he was interested in my pots. He'd seen them in the little gallery near where I live, and had picked up one of my cards. He was particularly interested in my glazes, you know, the colours I use, because I mix them myself."

"That's great!" said Ellie, feeling very pleased for her friend. "You're on your way."

Sophie bit her lip. "It *is* great," she said. "Or at least it will be if he really does buy one." She paused, and looked at Ellie. Her eyes were shining, and there was an undercurrent of nervous excitement in her voice. "Especially," she went on, "as I thought I recognized his name, he's called Mark Kettle. When I looked him up on the internet I discovered that he's a big name in the ceramics community as an avid collector of studio pottery."

"Really?"

"Yes. And he has a load of workshops he

rents to craftspeople, next to his museum, with a restaurant attached. He's a celebrated patron of the arts, Ellie...but..."

"What?" Ellie was puzzled. "Aren't you thrilled?"

"I just wish now that I hadn't told Flynn. He's gone totally over the top about it. He thinks I'm going to be famous overnight, a recognized studio potter who every gallery will want to collect. But it's not like that! I'm only just starting out. I'm thrilled that Mark Kettle has noticed me. It's fantastic, but if he is genuinely interested he'll want to see how I develop over the years. He's not going to rush off and announce to everyone in the art world that he's discovered a genius."

Ellie could see what Sophie meant. "Well, Flynn will get over it," she said, giving Sophie a hug. "He's proud of you, that's all."

"I know," said Sophie with a crooked smile. "I just wish he'd rein back his enthusiasm a bit.

It's all totally impossible to live up to." Her phone buzzed and she looked at the screen. "He's on his way down. Now please, Ellie, try not to encourage him."

Before Ellie could reply, Flynn appeared at the door with a beaming smile across his face. "Ellie! How are you? Have you heard Sophie's news?"

Ellie grinned back at him. "Yes I have. And I'm very well thank you, and glad to be back at *Heart*."

"Good. So, aren't you impressed? I am."

"Of course I am. It's great news!" said Ellie, trying to walk the narrow line between sounding too enthusiastic, which would annoy Sophie, and sounding totally disinterested, which would probably upset Flynn. "Guess what!" she added, trying to steer the subject away from Sophie and her pots. "I'm trying to get an interview with Charlie Daniels." But Flynn couldn't be deflected. He was opening his laptop as Ellie spoke, and didn't seem to have heard her at all.

"I bookmarked Mark Kettle's website," he said. "You won't believe how influential he is!" He put the laptop on the table, and opened it up. "He's an entrepreneur," he told Ellie. "And a patron of the arts. Apparently he's seen everywhere with famous people. He's *seriously* good news. Just imagine. Sophie could end up with *her* work in his collection of modern European studio pottery. How about that?"

Before Ellie could frame a sensible answer, Flynn clicked on another page in the website.

"You can read about him here."

Ellie was actually quite interested in finding out a bit about the man who might be buying one of Sophie's pots. If he really did have celebrity friends he might be involved in some things that the readers of *Heart* would like, and she could suggest him as someone else to interview for the magazine. But after quickly reading a bit about him she decided that he wasn't right for *Heart* readers. Apart from supporting the arts and craftspeople, his website said he enjoyed boats, especially large yachts, and had an ambition to sail around the world one day.

"He's such an important person in the art world," Flynn told Ellie as soon as she looked away from the screen.

"Yes," said Ellie. "He does seem to be. But it's good Sophie isn't getting too excited in case he doesn't buy a pot after all."

"You're as bad as she is!" said Flynn with a look of disappointment on his face. "It's good to be modest, but Sophie needs to be more confident. She ought to get out there and be seen, so he doesn't forget about her. After all, there's a lot of competition in the art world."

"I'm sure there is," said Ellie, unpacking her lunch and taking a bite out of the chicken wrap she'd made herself that morning.

"She needs to go to some really high-profile events."

"Who's going to invite *me* to high-profile events?" said Sophie, sounding rather fed up.

Flynn looked a little disconcerted, but then his face cleared. "You don't need invitations for *everything*," he told her. "There are things you could buy tickets for. They don't have to be arty events. Anywhere people might be who would be interested in your pots. You could take your cards and distribute them."

"Like I'm going to do that!" said Sophie. "You'll want me to go around sticking leaflets on car windscreens next. It's ridiculous."

"It's got to be better than sitting at home, waiting for people to come to you," he said. He sighed theatrically and looked at Ellie. "You see the problem I have with her?" he said.

"And you see the problem I have with *him*!" said Sophie with feeling. "For a start, someone *has* come to me. Mark Kettle! Isn't that good enough for you?" For a few seconds she looked really cross. Then she relented and went and gave Flynn a hug.

"I'm sorry," said Flynn, giving her a kiss. "You're right. I just want everyone to know about you. And I suppose I don't want you to risk losing famous Mr. Kettle."

"I'll keep my fingers crossed," said Ellie, trying to lighten the atmosphere. "I'm sure he'll *definitely* buy your pot. After all, he's seen and liked it...why wouldn't he?"

4
Drawing a blank

Back upstairs after lunch, Ellie looked at her emails. There was nothing from Charlie Daniels's agent, but the publisher had sent a brief message suggesting that Ellie might like to go to the author's website, as well as their own page advertising his books.

Well that's not very helpful, thought Ellie. *I've already done that!* She decided to have another look at the author's blog, but before she did that she opened another email that was waiting in her inbox. She didn't recognize the company it was from, but as the magazine's spam filters were pretty good she hoped it would be okay to open it. *It's some sort of agency,* she realized as the email opened with the heading, **SFB, Agent to the Stars** and an illustration of a shooting star trailing a tail of sparkles behind it.

Dear Ellie, the email began. *Pop Lowther has asked me to pass on this information that she promised you a while ago.*

Ellie's heart started thumping. She had almost given up hoping to hear from Pop. Ellie had interviewed the famous singing and modelling twins Pop and Lolly, and Pop had told her that she was going to start a new career. She couldn't tell her what it was then, in case things didn't work out, but Pop had promised to give the scoop to Ellie when she could. Ellie had heard nothing since, so this was very exciting.

Pop wanted you to know that her new venture will be to design a collection of casual clothes for a chain of high-street fashion stores. Details below. She will be making a statement about it soon, but is happy for your magazine to run the story as a scoop in your next issue if you wish. She also asked me to pass on her compliments and apologizes for not contacting you herself. She is in Morocco just now, on a modelling assignment.

Ellie read the email, then she read it again with a broad smile creeping across her face. This was *brilliant!* Francesca was bound to be pleased with her, and Angel ought to be as well. Every newspaper and magazine loved a scoop.

Ellie looked at the name at the bottom of the email. It was signed with a flourish, *Satin Fountain-Blowers*. She must be the "SFB" at the top of the email. Quickly, Ellie scrolled down to read the details with shaking hands. The heading said **Press Release**. It contained the name of the fashion stores, the name of an Italian designer who was working with Pop and a bit of information about them both. The press release was dated in the future, giving *Heart* enough time to get the information out before anyone else. Ellie closed the email carefully and got up. She wanted to reply, thanking Pop and Satin, but she thought it best to show Francesca first. She needed advice about scoops and how to use them.

"Francesca?" Ellie hovered by the Deputy Editor's desk.

"Found something on Charlie Daniels?"

"No. Sorry. Not yet." Ellie bit her lip to stop herself grinning too manically. "But I've just had an email I think you ought to see."

"Oh Ellie, can't it wait? I'm trying to get this article finished."

Ellie hesitated. "Well, it *will* wait I suppose."

Francesca looked up from her screen and sighed. "You've disturbed me now so I might as well look, otherwise I'll keep wondering what the problem is." She walked over to Ellie's desk and sat down. "Well?"

"I thought you should see this," said Ellie, reopening the email.

Francesca scanned it swiftly, scrolling down to read the press release. Then she turned to Ellie with an approving smile. "Well! You *are* turning out to be an asset. You must have made quite an impression on Pop and Lolly Lowther when you interviewed them. Have you replied yet?"

Ellie shook her head. "Not yet. I didn't want to risk messing it up by doing something stupid."

"Well good for you." Francesca looked very pleased. "Do reply, and thank Satin for letting you know. The sooner you reply, the better, then she'll know you've got the information okay." She looked back at the screen again. "The date is perfect for us. If they keep to that, we can definitely do a piece on this in the next issue of *Heart*, before it's released to anyone else. Once you've replied, why don't you write an account of how and why you were given the information, and show it to me. It would be great to have the story of how we came to get such a lovely scoop. Once that's done we can take it in and show Angel. What do you want, Piano?" she added as Piano joined them at Ellie's desk.

Piano was leaning against the window, looking down at Ellie with a suspicious expression on her face. Ellie wondered how much she'd overheard, but Piano wasn't about to let on.

"I wondered if Ellie had forgotten about Ferdinand," she said, looking down her nose. "Only it's getting rather late."

Ellie was sure that it was an excuse for Piano to come over to try and find out what Francesca and Ellie were looking so pleased about. Piano wouldn't usually remind Ellie of anything. She'd much rather look on, amused, while Ellie got told off. But she was right, it *was* past walk time for poor Ferdinand.

Ellie groaned inwardly, but to Piano she showed a smiling face. "I was just going to take him out!"

Ferdinand was Angel's little dog, and whenever Ellie was at the office it was her job to take him out for two or three walks each day. Unusually, Angel had taken him herself that morning, but now it was well after lunch, and if Ellie didn't hurry, Angel would be asking where she was; and if she did that it could lead to several other jobs, some of which Ellie would probably rather not do. Piano had actually done Ellie a real favour, because with all the excitement of the scoop from Satin, Ellie *had* forgotten all about the poor dog.

"Send your reply first," said Francesca. "It'll only take a moment."

"Okay," said Ellie. Francesca got up and gave Piano a quizzical look.

"Was there anything else you wanted to say?" she asked.

47

Ellie paid no attention to Piano's reply. She hurried to write an email back to Satin, making sure to thank her and asking her to pass on her grateful thanks to Pop. Then she pressed send.

Trying not to look as if she were hurrying, Ellie went and knocked on Angel's door. The Editor answered and Ellie went in. Angel looked at her with raised eyebrows as she took Ferdinand's lead from where it was hanging on the coat stand, and clipped it on to his collar.

"It's your job to clear up any puddles poor Ferdinand might make because you haven't taken him out in time," she said.

Ellie resisted the urge to wrinkle her nose in distaste. "Yes, Angel," she said, wondering if Piano had ever been given that job, and feeling determined that it would never happen to her. "Come on then, Ferdinand," she said, and the little dog jumped out of his basket and ran to the door, tugging Ellie after him.

Ferdinand didn't really like going in the lift,

so Ellie picked him up and carried him while they were going down. "Where shall we go then?" she asked him as they went out onto the street. "How about the park?"

The park was actually the only place to take a dog, unless he was going for grooming, at Pamper Your Pets. It wasn't far, and soon they reached the specially enclosed area that was set aside for dogs. It was a warm day, so Ellie sat on a bench, thinking about the celebrities on her list, while Ferdinand sniffed about and said hello to the other dogs being walked in the park. Ellie could remember from earlier visits a large poodle that he liked to play with, and two very friendly little scruffy terriers, a bit like him, that he enjoyed rough and tumble games with as well. Today the poodle wasn't there, but the terriers arrived at the same time as Ellie and Ferdinand. Their middle-aged owner joined her on the bench.

"Is that Ferdinand?" she asked, pointing to

where he was playing with her two dogs.

"Yes," said Ellie. "I'm exercising him for my boss."

"I thought it must be him," said the woman. "My two enjoy playing with him so much. He's more their size than most of the dogs that come here. And he's so good natured."

"Yes, he is," said Ellie with a smile. It was rather nice to have another dog walker to talk to.

"I think I remember seeing you a while ago," said the woman. "But it's usually a girl with long blonde hair who brings him."

"That's Piano." Ellie explained about school, and how she dog walked during the holidays for the editor at *Heart* magazine.

"Ah. That explains it," said the woman. "Is Ferdinand the only dog you walk?"

"Yes," said Ellie. "And most of the time at work I'm fetching coffee, although I have done a couple of interviews."

The woman looked surprised. "That must be exciting," she said. Then she blew out a puff of air. "Phew! It's warm today," she said, changing the subject and fanning her face with her hand.

"Yes, it is," agreed Ellie. "But the dogs don't seem to mind."

The woman smiled. "No, they don't, do they."

Ferdinand and her two dogs were having great fun chasing each other.

For a while longer Ellie and the woman sat quietly on the bench, enjoying the sun. Then the woman looked at her. "Well, sorry to spoil your Ferdinand's fun, but I must go." She stood up and called to her dogs. "Come on, Beastly. Snappit, come here. Time to go home."

Ellie wanted to giggle at their names. They were gentle little animals, and neither name seemed to suit the dogs, but maybe that was the point. Some people did like silly names for their pets. But the woman obviously needed to get home, and Ferdinand was leaping about, encouraging her dogs to misbehave. To be helpful, Ellie lunged at Ferdinand, and caught one of the woman's dogs too. She put Ferdinand's lead on, and stood on it so he couldn't run away. Then she held the woman's little dog while the other waited meekly to have his lead put on, now the game had ended. The little silver tag on the collar of the dog she was holding caught Ellie's eye. It was most unusual, being in the shape of an open book instead of a round disc or tube with an address in.

"What a lovely tag!" said Ellie. She caught hold of it and looked at the name on it: *Snappit*. "You're not at all snappy, are you?" she laughed, stroking the friendly little dog. Ellie turned the tag over. *If found please return to...*

"Thank you so much!" To Ellie's surprise the woman practically snatched Snappit out of Ellie's arms and hurriedly put on his lead.

"I'm so sorry," she apologized. "But I've just remembered something. I'm very late. I simply must go. So sorry!"

Without another word she got up and left the dog enclosure. Ellie watched as she rushed out of the park without a backward glance.

"Well, Ferdi," she said, feeling a bit put out. "I hope she makes it to whatever she's late for. You were naughty, leading those dogs astray. Come on. It's time we went back now too."

By the time Ellie and Ferdinand got back to the office it was quite late. There wasn't really time for her to write about her scoop, so Francesca suggested she leave it until the morning. "Now you've thanked Satin, it'll keep for a day," she said. "And anyway, Angel has gone out, so you can't go and tell her about it now. Why don't you take the post down to Sophie to be franked? Then it will be time to go home. It'll be better to write your piece in the morning when you're fresh."

"Good idea," said Ellie at once.

"One piece of advice," added Francesca as Ellie picked up her bag. "Don't tell a soul about your email from Satin. Not even your best friend. The more people who know, the more leaky the scoop will become. It's amazing how these things get out. Once we've gone to press and the magazine is out it'll be fine, but until then it has to stay in our office."

"Okay," said Ellie. It was a shame she wouldn't be able to tell Hannah or Sophie, but she could see what Francesca meant. Secrets passed around like Chinese Whispers very soon stopped being secrets and became inaccurate as well. That sort of thing happened at school all the time, but Ellie was determined that her secret should remain one, until it was time to let it out. She collected up all the post from the Editorial Department and headed down to give it to Sophie.

"Has Flynn stopped going on about Mark

Kettle?" she said as she handed the post to her friend.

Sophie frowned. "Well I haven't seen him since lunch," she said. "He's gone quiet for the moment. I'm sure he still has plans though, probably to be my marketing manager, as soon as I can afford to leave work here and concentrate on being a pot-making genius."

"Oh don't be cross with him." Ellie hated to see her friends squabble.

"I just wish he'd let me do my things my way," Sophie sighed, then her face cleared and she smiled. "Anyway, how did you enjoy your first day back?"

"It's been good," said Ellie, regretting even more that she couldn't share her most exciting news. "But I'm no further forward with Charlie Daniels, in spite of following your advice. I'm beginning to think he's a real recluse. No one seems to have met him, or know anything about him. I'm not going to give up yet though. I hate to be beaten."

"Well you've got nothing to lose," said Sophie.

Ellie laughed. "I know. And Francesca must think I've got a little bit of a chance, otherwise she wouldn't have suggested it." Ellie turned to go. "See you tomorrow."

While she was waiting for the bus a text came in from Hannah. *Can I come round tonight? I've got cans of beans swimming before my eyes!*

Ellie laughed. Hannah's job at her aunt's shop seemed to be getting to her already.

Sure!

Ellie clutched her phone in one hand and her bag in the other as she climbed on the bus, reminding herself to steer clear of any mention of Pop and Lolly Lowther.

Great! I badly need fun. See you at 7?

Ellie sent her one word back.

Yep.

She had the perfect activity for a jaded Hannah; dreaming up more celebrities for her list!

In Ellie's room that evening the two girls did enjoy discussing people for *Heart* to feature.

"The in-house list had some people on it I didn't know," said Ellie. "There's a singer on the internet, but I couldn't very well listen to his songs in the office. Let's see what he sounds like. *Heart* must think he's going to be the next big thing."

Once they'd done that and been duly impressed by him they tried to think of more big names that everyone would want to read about.

"That rugby player...Nick Houseman," said Hannah. "He's gorgeous!"

"Yes," agreed Ellie. "And talking about gorgeous, I wanted to add Al from Zone One, but Francesca wouldn't let me."

Hannah laughed. "You've already written about his band, and they've done a shoot for *Heart*. Besides, you can't interview just one member of a band!"

"I don't see why not," said Ellie wistfully, thinking how wonderful it would be to get Al all to herself. "But Francesca more or less said the same thing."

"She's right," said Hannah firmly. "You can't interview people just because you fancy them. It's not professional."

Reluctantly, Ellie tried to come up with a different name. "Kurt Draagan," she said.

"Now he *is* a good idea," said Hannah, who was sprawled on Ellie's bed. "He was brilliant in *The Vampire Sleeps*." She closed her eyes and smiled. "He has that smouldering look... fantastic!"

"Now who's being unprofessional?" said Ellie.

Hannah opened her eyes and grinned at

Ellie. "I don't have to be professional," she said. "It's not my list, and I won't be doing any of the interviews."

"I don't know how many I'll manage to fit in over this holiday," said Ellie thoughtfully. "By the time I've got *some* of these people to agree to an interview I expect we'll be back at school. But if it's a yes from Kurt Draagan, I'll make sure they arrange it so I can be there, even if they have to wait until Christmas!"

"What about one of the weather girls on TV?" suggested Hannah. "Neesha Abbots for instance. She was on that Reality TV show, *Mix Up*. Remember? They don't *all* have to be totally fanciable boys."

"No," said Ellie with a laugh. "They don't, do they? And a few more girls would be good. Who else is there?"

"Mellita," said Hannah straight away. "She's so cool. I love her latest album."

They soon had a good long list of people,

and Ellie was sure Francesca would be pleased with the extras they'd come up with. "I'll owe you if any of yours get chosen," she said. "But for the moment I'm concentrating on Charlie Daniels, and he's proving tricky."

She explained the problem to Hannah. "Well maybe he just doesn't have any publicity shots," said Hannah. "There wasn't a picture of him on the cover of the books, was there?"

"You're right," said Ellie. "Perhaps he just hates having his picture taken." She took the first book in the trilogy down from her shelf and studied it. "This is the film version though," she mused. "It must have come out with a different cover on originally."

Hannah looked at her. "What are you getting at?"

"Well." Ellie scratched her head. "Isn't it hardback books that usually have the author's photograph on? Maybe when the books *first* came out there *was* a picture."

"But who would have the hardbacks?" said Hannah. "I can't think of anyone."

"I can," said Ellie.

"Who?"

"Not a who, a what. The library!"

Hannah grinned at Ellie. "Good thinking."

"I'll go tomorrow," said Ellie. "There must be a library not too far from work. I can look online to see where the nearest one is. If I could just find a photograph of Charlie Daniels it would make him more real somehow. That's great, Hannah. Thanks for your help."

"You thought of it," said Hannah with a laugh.

"But I never would have done if we hadn't been discussing him together," said Ellie. She put the book on the bed. "There's a fab competition on the publisher's website," she said. "Check it out."

"Okay," said Hannah, swinging her legs off Ellie's bed and standing up. "I must go now.

I need my beauty sleep. I've been stacking shelves for Aunt Bella all day, and my arms are aching. You get to chill out in a library, while I get to build up my biceps."

"But just think how toned you'll look on the beach," said Ellie with a giggle.

"And maybe Kurt Draagan will turn up," added Hannah. "If so, I'll put in a word for you."

"Thanks!"

Ellie saw Hannah out and then went back to her room. She tossed her notebook onto her desk. Then she picked it up again. Did her dad have any comments that might help? She paused at the first page, as she always did. *You can do this!* was inspiring, but she wanted more. Her father had been a great journalist. He must have known all the tricks of the trade.

Ellie yawned as she turned over the pages. It was too late to be thinking of this now. She ought to go to sleep and start again in the morning, when she was fresh and clear-headed. Then she came to a page that made her stop. *Don't overlook anything.* She read it again. Her dad had often been abroad in violent situations, reporting for his newspaper. Overlooking things then probably could be very dangerous. But Mum had said how careful he always was. Sometimes though, however careful you were bad things could happen, and eventually, her father had lost his life. At least Ellie didn't have to worry about danger in her job. All the same, the advice was sound. A good journalist would certainly try not to ignore anything, in case it was important.

Well…she stifled another yawn. She would make notes on this page, to keep herself on track. She wrote the next day's date on the page and marked it. Tomorrow she would attempt to build up a profile on Charlie Daniels, and she would try especially hard not to miss anything, in case it might prove useful. She snuggled down under her duvet and, just before she closed her eyes, she saw her father's black notebook waiting on her desk. She smiled sleepily. *Thanks, Hannah, and thanks, Dad.*

5
A breakthrough and heartbreak

First thing in the morning, before breakfast, Ellie looked online to see where the nearest library was to the *Heart* offices. If she got off the bus a couple of stops earlier than usual she could easily visit one, so she emailed Francesca's office address while she ate her breakfast. Francesca always started work early.

Okay if I visit library on the way to work today? Might have a lead.

It wasn't long before she got an answer.

Fine. See you a bit later.

The librarian was very helpful. "We do have

a couple of the hardbacks," she said when Ellie asked. "I'll just see if any of them are in."

Ellie waited anxiously while the librarian looked on her computer. "We should have one on the shelf. I'm afraid it's volume two, so if you haven't read the first one you might not want it."

"That's all right," said Ellie. "I don't actually want to read it."

The librarian gave her a startled look. "Really? Well, it should be over here." She led the way to the shelf and picked it out immediately. "This series is so popular," she said. "Since the film came out we can't keep up with the demand."

Ellie wasn't listening. She looked on the back, but there was no author picture. She looked inside too, but to her disappointment she drew a blank there as well. There were some notes about the author, but they were almost as brief as the ones in the paperback version she had: *The Fanghurst Trilogy attracted unprecedented excitement when it was first offered for publication, and has already been sold to over a dozen countries. Charlie Daniels lives in London, and is now working on a prequel,* Fanghurst Born.

Ellie closed the book. "Thank you," she said politely, handing it back to the librarian. "I just wanted to see if there was an author picture, but there isn't."

The librarian turned the book over in her hands. "You're right," she said. "Publishers like pictures of the author as a rule. I expect it helps a bit at bookshop signings. I wonder why they didn't do it for this author?"

"I don't know," said Ellie.

She decided to walk the rest of the way to work. *Well, at least I've found out that he lives in London!* she thought to herself. *That's something.*

It wasn't that far to walk, and it was a lovely

morning. But nearby there was a bookshop, and on a whim, Ellie went in.

She very quickly found a pile of the paperbacks and took one to the counter. "Do you know if Charlie Daniels does book signings?" she asked. "Or if he's going to some time?"

The assistant held out her hand for the book, but Ellie held onto it. "I don't want to buy it," she said. "I was just wondering about book signings."

The assistant shrugged. "I've got no idea," he said. "You could try the publisher. They might know. I haven't heard of an author tour though."

"Thanks," said Ellie, putting the book back on the stack. As soon as she had finished the piece she had to write about Pop's new fashion range she'd phone the publisher. Surely, with so much publicity about the film, Charlie Daniels would want to do a book tour? If it were Ellie, she knew that she would!

"Any progress in your quest to interview our illusive author?" said Francesca when Ellie arrived at work.

"Not really," said Ellie. "Though I now know he lives in London." She hesitated. "And I'm going to ring the publisher once I've written the piece about Pop Lowther."

"Good for you," said Francesca. "It's great he's in London. That will make an interview much easier to set up if you can make contact. Well done!"

Ellie got straight on with her piece about Pop's new venture, and soon had an article to show Francesca.

"She says she wants to design clothes she loves wearing herself," Ellie told Francesca. "And she mentions Carlotta Bellini, who she'll be working with, as a huge influence, so I did a bit of digging on the internet and found out a bit more about her. I've attached that to the article in case you're interested."

"Excellent work, Ellie," said Francesca, looking very pleased. "Give me a few minutes to edit it and then we'll go and show Angel."

Soon they were both heading for Angel's office, and Piano was trying to look as if she wasn't interested, but Ellie could see that she was watching their every move. Ellie had to fight the urge to giggle. She could imagine the shocked expression on Piano's face when she found out what Ellie had written. Piano so often liked to make Ellie feel as if she was a hopeless case, but Ellie was certain she wasn't going to be made to feel like an underdog today!

Angel was a formidable Editor in Chief, but Francesca never seemed to be in awe of her. She knocked, went straight in and up to Angel's desk. Angel looked happy to see her, but not so pleased that Ellie had come with her.

"What's up?" said Angel.

"Ellie has been given a scoop by Pop Lowther," said Francesca without any preamble.

"Her agent has sent Ellie an advance copy of the press release so that we can publish the item first."

"Really?" Angel looked at Ellie with her steely blue eyes, but they held interest and respect, not ire. "And why has she opted to give you this exclusivity?"

"Umm...well..." Ellie tried to explain. "We seemed to get on really well when I interviewed them during my work experience here, and she told me then that she was looking into a new venture and would let me know when she was ready to announce it. I think she was trying to help me with being a journalist," she added, trying to be totally honest.

Angel nodded. "I remember that article, and the hint in it of information to come." She smiled at Ellie. "You obviously have empathy, and that goes a long way with people. If they feel you're on their side they tend to open up more. Well done. It looks as if you have the makings of a fine journalist. What is the scoop, by the way?"

"It's about Pop going into clothes design for a big fashion store," said Ellie, thrilled by Angel's praise. "I've done an article." She offered Angel the printed-out article but Angel waved it away. "That's all right, Francesca can cast an eye over it." She looked at her deputy. "But we'll need to discuss where it will go in the magazine," she said. "Maybe that piece on the film actor...let's talk it over in about twenty minutes, Francesca. I need to make a phone call just now. Well done," she added vaguely in Ellie's direction. "I look forward to reading it in due course."

Angel was already starting to make the call as Ellie and Francesca left, but Ellie didn't mind about the interview being so brief. She knew how busy the Editor in Chief was.

"Well," said Francesca as she closed the door behind them and they made their way back to their desks. "What a good start to your summer. What else are you thinking of impressing us with?"

Ellie couldn't help laughing. She could practically hear Piano's ears flapping. "Well I'm going to get on with tracking down Charlie Daniels in a minute, if that's okay, but I need to give you this first." She handed Francesca the list of celebrity names that she and Hannah had thought of the night before. "I don't know if you'll want to use any of them, but I thought it was worth noting them down."

Francesca laughed too. "Thanks, Ellie. It's great to see such enthusiasm."

"So is it okay if I get on with Charlie Daniels now?"

"So far as I'm concerned, as long as you remember the coffee run and the dog walking, you can spend the rest of today on it if you want. You won't be able to spend this much time on most of the names on the list, but then you shouldn't need to. And I do think it's worth pursuing this one for a bit longer. Just make sure you clear it with me before you actually *do* anything. Okay? I'd hate you to get into trouble, or us for that matter."

"Okay. Thanks, Francesca."

"And, Ellie, don't worry if you draw a blank. I won't be annoyed or surprised if you do, but it could make a really interesting, and different interview for the magazine if you could pull it off. Just keep your eyes and ears open, and if you can piece anything together about him let me know."

"I'll do my best," said Ellie, feeling pleased at what Francesca had said. The pressure was off, but in a way that made her even more determined to track the author down.

She sat down and opened her laptop. First she went back to the publisher's website and took down their number. Then she pulled her notebook out of her bag. When she phoned she'd need to write down anything that might be useful. She took a couple of deep breaths and dialled the number.

"Bishop and Stoker Publishers. Which department would you like?"

"Um…" She wasn't ready for that. "I need to talk to someone who would know about author signings…" she said, scrambling to try and sound as if she knew exactly what she was talking about. "And about Ch—" But the receptionist interrupted.

"Putting you through."

The phone rang for ages, and Ellie was beginning to think that no one was going to answer it, but just as she was about to put it down and try again, someone picked up.

"Hello?"

The girl's voice sounded very young, and Ellie could hear someone else speaking in the background. Just as Ellie was about to explain what she wanted to know, the sound became muffled, as if someone had half put their hand over the receiver. Then the girl's voice became clear again. "Sorry about that. This is the Publicity Department. Can I help you?"

"I hope so," said Ellie. "I work for *Heart* magazine, and I wondered if Charlie Daniels is going to do any book signings, or appearances... that sort of thing."

"Oh." There was a pause. "Well I doubt it, but it's not my place to say anything about Charlie Daniels."

Ellie felt puzzled. "Why not?"

"Well I'm just helping out with posters and stuff. I don't usually answer the phone."

Ellie sighed. "Well can I speak to someone who *is* able to talk about Charlie Daniels then?"

"She's in a meeting."

"Well..." Ellie really didn't want to give up. "Can you at least get someone to send me a publicity photo?"

"Oh dear..." The girl on the other end of the phone sounded quite agitated. "There was a picture, but then they changed their minds... There aren't any here. And I don't think there will be a tour...though a tour would be so cool. I think it's a shame," she added. "With the film and everything. They should do it...but you'll need to call back later, to speak to Jackie Turner. She's in charge of that campaign, but I'm sure you won't be able to interview the author. Maybe one day, but not yet. Okay?"

"Okay," said Ellie slowly.

She put the phone down and frowned. What on earth had all that been about? Surely a Publicity Department should be offering to send out all sorts of stuff. But this girl had been hopeless. And what was up with Charlie Daniels that he wouldn't give interviews, refused to have any photographs taken, and didn't intend, so far as she could tell, to go on an author tour? Why on earth not? The second film would soon be released, and loads of people would want to buy signed copies of his books, and meet him, but he wouldn't do it. How bizarre.

While Ellie was pondering, Sophie appeared with the post, and dropped it on the reception desk for Debbie Wu to distribute around the office. Ellie didn't expect any post, but she gave Sophie a cheerful wave. To Ellie's surprise, the post girl didn't seem her usual cheerful self. She hardly raised any sort of a smile for Ellie, and immediately Ellie began to worry. She hoped her friends weren't still at odds over Sophie's pots. She decided to call in to see Sophie on the way back from walking Ferdinand.

"Come on, Ferdinand," she told Angel's dog as he hesitated at the open lift. "It's quite safe, you know, and I'm not going to pick you up today. If I do, you'll make this jumper all hairy."

In the dog section of the park, they were just in time to see the two little terriers disappearing out of the gate with their mistress.

"Never mind," said Ellie, giving Ferdinand a pat. "And look! Here's Thompson the poodle!"

Thompson's owner was a middle-aged man. He never seemed very keen to let his large black poodle associate with Ferdinand. Maybe he thought Angel's little dog too scruffy to play with his elegant, high-stepping poodle. Ellie wondered if his attitude would change if he realized that Ferdi was actually owned by a woman who was a high flyer and at least as elegant as his poodle! But today she didn't wonder, or let the two dogs play for long. As soon as Ferdinand had run around for a while she called him back and slipped his lead onto his collar.

When they got back to the office building Ellie went down to the basement to see Sophie.

She was taping up a small parcel, and Ellie was dismayed to see that her eyes were red, as if she'd been crying.

"What's the matter?" she said.

Sophie finished the parcel and pushed it to one side. "Oh, Flynn and I had a stupid argument last night, and now we're not talking and..." She looked at Ellie and sighed. "Ever since I was contacted by Mark Kettle things have gone wrong. I just wish I'd never heard of him." She gave Ellie a wobbly smile. "Don't worry. It'll be all right in the end I expect. And there's nothing you can do," she added as Ellie started to speak. "We'll probably make up this evening, and everything will be back to normal by tomorrow. Every relationship has its ups and downs you know."

Ellie supposed Sophie must be right, but it made her feel sad to think that two such lovely people had fallen out. It was obvious that Sophie didn't want to talk about it any more, so

Ellie gave her a hug and took Ferdinand back upstairs.

Back at her desk, Ellie googled "Charlie Daniels" again. Seeing Sophie so upset had unsettled her, and she was finding it hard to concentrate. She scrolled absently down the first page of websites that the search engine had found. At the bottom it told her that it had found 250,000 pages. She sighed. She needed to refine her search. She'd never plough through all those pages in a million years. Ellie thought for a moment and then added *author* to the search. That was a bit better...105,000 results came up this time. Even so, there were far too many. She could ignore the first fifty. She'd looked at those already. And maybe all the others would prove to be useless. But somewhere there might be a phone number, or an address. Her father's phrase, not to overlook anything sprang into her mind. The internet did hold an awful lot of random information.

How could she best access it? Then a thought struck her.

Everyone searches pages on the internet from the first one and works backwards. What if I started at the back? There might be some useful things hidden on an old page that no one looks at any more.

It only took a couple of minutes to speed through to the last page of results, by skipping as many as the search engine would allow.

Damn!

The last page didn't yield any results about Charlie Daniels at all. They were all web pages where the words "Author", "Daniels", or "Charlie" had been picked out, but they didn't refer to the Charlie Daniels she wanted to read about. Slowly, Ellie flipped back through the results, looking for one that might actually be about him. A couple of pages back she spied one. It was an obscure blog by someone who she'd never heard of before, and it was four years old, but it had been tagged by the internet search engine as having a reference to her man, and there was always a chance that it might yield something. Ellie opened her notebook, picked up her pen and prepared to concentrate.

The blog was called *Paws for Thought* and it was by someone called Matt Budgeon. Most of the entries were about Matt's dogs, and the dogs owned by his friends. *So how does Charlie Daniels figure in all this stuff?* Ellie asked herself. The only way to find out was to read it. The latest entry was called "Names".

It's amazing how unimaginative people can be with their dog names, read Ellie. *If they don't choose human names (a total cop-out I think) they go for ones that are ridiculous. Why name a dog Badger, or Moth? Keep a badger, if you want a badger for goodness' sake!*

Ellie found herself giggling. This Matt Budgeon person sounded very grumpy. She wondered if he was still blogging, and if so, if anyone ever read it.

The best names usually go in pairs, she read. *Pepper and Salt, Rhubarb and Custard, Snippet and Snappit, Cut and Paste. In my opinion, if you want to keep a dog, keep two, and like my old friend, the maybe soon to be famous scribbler Charlie Daniels (wot a name, wink wink!!) give them imaginative names, not cop-out ones. Just make sure they're the same age, or one day, old Rhubarb's companion will pass on, and then you'll be left looking for a new Custard.*

Ellie caught her breath. She'd found something. Charlie Daniels kept dogs, and two of them at that. And this was a blog by one of his friends, who thought he had given them imaginative names! The blog might prove very useful, if it was still going. She could look in a moment. Quickly, she scribbled down what she'd found, feeling rather pleased with herself, although it didn't seem to be leading her anywhere yet. So now...why did one of the names she'd just read ring a faint bell in her head?

Ellie leaned back in her chair and closed her eyes. She was sure she'd heard one of those names recently. Was it on another website about Charlie Daniels? She'd looked at so many. Then Francesca disturbed her.

"Sorry?" Ellie opened her eyes and looked at Francesca standing by her desk.

"I wondered if you were going shopping during your lunch break. Or if you could get something for me when you take Ferdinand out this afternoon. I need you to go to the stationer's. I've got an urgent deadline, I'm just not going to be able to get out."

"Oh! Umm..." It was so annoying to be interrupted. She was sure she'd never remember now. Then, suddenly, she did. "Ferdinand? Ferdinand! His friend, Snappit. That's it!"

"I'm sorry."

"No, it's not you, Francesca. Sorry. I was just trying to remember something, but I was thinking the wrong way. It wasn't anything to do with Charlie Daniels. Snappit is Ferdinand's friend."

Then Ellie stopped, as a sudden, huge, scary, tremendous thought swooped into her head. What if Snappit and Snippit were the blogger's dogs, or maybe even Charlie Daniels's? And what if Snippit had died...and he'd got Beastly instead? After all, the blog was four years old. And Snappit was hardly a common dog's name. And what about the dog tag she'd so admired on Snappit's collar – that little silver book. Might that be significant?

Ellie tried to stay calm, but it wasn't easy. Could Charlie Daniels be much closer than she thought? After all, she now knew he lived in this city, and owned two dogs. There were lots of places to take dogs in London, but few parks in the centre of town were quite as well set up for them and their owners as this one. He, or his dog walker had to take them *somewhere.* She remembered holding the tag in her hand, and the woman virtually snatching Snappit out of her arms. Had she really been late for an appointment, or was it that she didn't want Ellie to read the address or phone number on the tag? And why would someone not want their address known unless it was important? Was that woman Charlie Daniels's dog walker ...as Ellie was Ferdinand's...or was she the blogger...or maybe even Charlie Daniels's wife?

The thought was so huge that for a moment Ellie couldn't take it in. Ideas started bouncing round inside her head like a bumblebee on a windowpane, and she fought to control them and calm down. She would take Ferdinand at his usual time, when Beastly and Snappit would be there. She could simply ask the woman if she was connected to Charlie Daniels, but somehow, if she was, Ellie had the feeling that she'd deny it, to protect him...from the possibility of journalists turning up on his doorstep perhaps. It would be better to catch one of the dogs again, so she could look on a tag. There might be a phone number... It was worth a try. Of course Francesca had told her to discuss it before she did anything. But surely she meant before she actually phoned or went to an address. Just walking in the park and chatting to other dog owners about their dogs wasn't actually *doing* anything...was it?

Ellie didn't want to confide in Francesca. She was afraid she'd laugh at her theory...and maybe even forbid her to pick up either of the little dogs again and risk angering their owner. But most owners loved talking about their dogs, and having them admired... There was the woman's rather odd attitude, the silver book tag and the name...maybe it was too much to hope that the dogs actually belonged to the elusive Charlie Daniels, but Angel had seemed to think Ellie was the sort of person others might confide in. If the woman was a friend of his, Ellie might be able to talk her way into meeting him. It might, if she was very lucky, all come right.

6
Back to the park

It was impossible for Ellie to sit calmly at her desk. Instead, she decided to go for an early lunch, and to the stationer's for Francesca at the same time. Often, she ate lunch with Sophie and sometimes Flynn as well, but she felt too awkward to do that today. Besides, it would probably be better to leave them to work out their differences. Having her hanging around was unlikely to help, so with some relief at having made that decision, Ellie took her bag and left the office.

She went to the stationer's first. Francesca kept a combined notebook and diary personal organizer, which you could add pages to. Ellie thought it was a rather old-fashioned way to keep up to date. She used the diary on her phone, but Francesca liked to write her appointments down, and Ellie had to admit the green, leather-covered organizer did look pretty cool. Francesca wanted a packet of refills for her to-do list, and it took a matter of minutes for Ellie to buy the size she wanted.

Once that was done, Ellie felt at a bit of a loose end. She didn't need any shopping herself, and she found herself being drawn in the direction of the park, even though she didn't have Ferdinand with her. She had a sandwich in her bag, and a bottle of water…she might as well eat it there as anywhere else.

As she ate her lunch Ellie kept a close eye on all the people and dogs going in and out. But by the time she'd finished her food there had been no sign of the dogs she'd half hoped to see. She got up with a sigh, and shook the crumbs from her clothes for the sparrows.

Back at work, Ellie changed into her office shoes and stowed her outdoor ones in the cupboard in the lobby. She was straightening up again when an odd sight met her eyes. The reception desk was right ahead of her, and leaning on it, talking to Debbie Wu, was Flynn. Lots of girls in the offices liked to flirt with Flynn. He *was* very good-looking, so it was hardly surprising. It was a bit of a joke with Sophie. Sometimes she teased him about it, and Flynn took it all good-humouredly. But Ellie had never seen him respond to a girl's approach. He'd never shown the slightest interest in anyone except Sophie. He'd always been totally loyal to her, so far as Ellie knew, but there he was, leaning in towards Debbie, and beaming all over his face, as if he thought her the best thing he'd seen for ages. Ellie's heart gave a jump. What was he *doing*? Surely he realized that smiling so much at Debbie would only encourage her? Then her heart gave another flip and sank to her feet. Maybe he *wanted* to encourage her. Maybe his falling out with Sophie was worse than she'd thought.

Ellie really didn't want to walk past them. She felt embarrassed. What could she say? Should she look disapproving? She was sure she'd be unable to show any other expression on her face, but it was really none of her business. Flynn and Sophie had to sort their own lives out between them. It didn't matter how loyal she felt towards Sophie, there was nothing Ellie could do about Flynn's behaviour.

Taking a deep breath, Ellie marched towards the reception desk. She had decided to avert her face, and say nothing at all, but as she drew close, Flynn spoke to her. "Hi, Ellie!"

Ellie mumbled a greeting and strode on to her desk. She sat down and folded her arms. He wasn't even *ashamed*! Presumably he didn't care that she'd seen what he was up to. How *could* he?

To distract herself, Ellie began to read the latest article that Piano had written. But the words danced about on the screen. She was so cross for Sophie that she read the same sentence three times without it making any sense at all. Defeated, she flipped to another screen and glared at some pictures of handbags for a few minutes. When she was feeling a bit calmer she glanced over to the reception desk. Flynn had gone, and Debbie was sitting there as if nothing had happened at all.

Ellie took the packet of organizer paper over to Francesca's desk. Francesca wasn't there. She must be at one of the frequent meetings she had with Angel. Ellie wondered if they were talking about her celebrity list. Probably not. It was getting near publication day, so they were almost certainly going through the pages of the next issue, making sure everything was as perfect as possible, including her scoop of course. It would be fantastic to see that in the magazine. Piano hadn't said anything to Ellie about that, though she must know about it now it had become part of the next issue.

Piano was at her desk. "I've got a job for you if you're at a loose end," she said.

Ellie started. "Actually I've got lots to do, thanks," she said.

Piano looked at her sourly. "Yes, well I could see you earlier, trying to pretend you were a proper journalist. A lucky break with Pop Lowther, and a little bit of encouragement from Francesca and you think you've arrived."

Ellie couldn't help herself. "So aren't scoops part of being a journalist?" she said sweetly.

Piano did her usual eye-rolling thing, as if Ellie was totally clueless.

"If you *have* got anything useful to do, get on with it. And don't forget our coffee," she added in a huff.

"I *know*," Ellie called back over her shoulder. She was sure she must sound like a grumpy child, but Piano made her feel like one. And seeing Flynn with Debbie had really unsettled her. Still, it could have been worse. Imagine if he'd been chatting up Piano?

At that thought, in spite of her concern for Sophie, Ellie wanted to giggle. Flynn wouldn't last ten seconds with Piano. She would spend all her time trying to boss him about, and he wouldn't like that one bit!

Determined not to give Piano an opportunity to give her a job to do, Ellie did a search for the blogger who had mentioned the author's dogs. He hadn't kept his blog going for very long, but all the old posts still remained. She started reading them eagerly. There might be something else buried there that would be useful.

There was an email address for him, so Ellie started to write a message. Then she paused. If Charlie Daniels didn't like the media, and it felt very much as if he didn't, surely any approach from a magazine would immediately get deleted? Maybe it would be better to send a message from her hotmail address, so it didn't look as if she was working for *Heart*? If she could get the blogger on her side, and if he was a friend of Charlie Daniels, maybe, just maybe, she could reassure him that an interview with her didn't mean that the writer would lose his privacy. Ellie had the uncomfortable feeling that Francesca might not think it a very ethical approach, but she told herself that she would be totally honest as soon as she had a dialogue going. The blogger didn't really need to know that she and *Heart* were connected, not to begin with anyway. She decided to try cunning, and so she suggested that she had something to tell Charlie Daniels that he might like to hear. She spent ages wording her message, trying to make it sound as tempting as possible. Even if he thought it was spam and simply deleted it, well, at least she would have tried her best.

After hesitating for a moment she took a deep breath and pressed send. She could always try again using the magazine email, though she didn't have much hope that the direct approach would work.

Ellie was sure she'd done all she could for now, and looking at the time on her screen she realized she ought to go and fetch the coffee, otherwise she'd be late taking Ferdinand to meet his friends Snappit and Beastly. All her efforts to remain calm deserted her as she allowed herself to think about it. She'd have to use a huge dose of empathy to put the woman at her ease. If she succeeded, and the woman *was* connected with Charlie Daniels, and if she *did* get a contact number, Francesca would be totally impressed. As for Piano...well, Ellie would then have *two* scoops instead of just the one. That would teach Piano to be so irritating! Although Ellie had to admit to herself that there were an awful lot of ifs and maybes in this scenario. It was a very long shot indeed.

She tidied her desk, closed the lid of her laptop and went to get the coffee. Francesca and Angel were still in Angel's office, their heads together, as they put the final touches to the next issue of *Heart*. Ellie put their coffees carefully on Angel's desk and took Ferdinand's lead from the coat stand.

"No, Ferdinand—" Angel put out a restraining hand as she caught sight of her dog leaving his basket. Then she noticed Ellie with his lead. "Oh all right. Is it that time already?"

"It's almost three," said Ellie.

"Yes, yes. Go on then." Angel waved her away. "Francesca, we need to do something with this page. It's not lively enough."

Francesca reached for her coffee with a nod of thanks to Ellie. "How about lifting the background colour a bit?" she said.

Angel shook her head impatiently. "That wouldn't be enough. No, we really need to emphasize this section here. Let's try putting the illustration in a box."

Ellie clipped Ferdinand's lead on and left them to it. She closed the door quietly behind her and then she and Ferdinand hurried away. Ellie felt her excitement mounting at every step they took towards the park. Maybe Snappit and Beastly's walker would ask Ellie to keep an eye on them while she went to the loo, or to get an ice cream. It was a lovely day. In fact, maybe Ellie ought to get herself an ice cream, and encourage the woman to do the same. A couple of minutes alone with that silver book tag would tell her all she needed to know.

All of a sudden she wished she'd got a ball for the dogs to chase. It would be so simple to look at the tag when the dogs came back to have the ball thrown again. But it was too late for that now. And Francesca had only given Ellie the rest of the day to make a breakthrough. She *had* to find out if there was a connection.

Full of excitement and enthusiasm, Ellie and Ferdinand entered the dog enclosure. Ellie looked about for the two little dogs, but they weren't there. She bagged the best bench as soon as an elderly man with a Labrador vacated it, and felt very pleased with herself. She was in the right position, there was room on the bench for Snappit and Beastly's owner, and the ice cream kiosk was nearby. Everything was in place.

But it was hard waiting. Ferdinand was fine. So far as *he* was concerned it was just a normal visit to the park, but for Ellie it was agony. The minutes ticked by painfully slowly, and in the end she had to tell herself to stop looking at her watch. But time did pass, and eventually Ferdinand came and lay at Ellie's feet. He'd never done that before. Usually she had to call him to her, but it seemed he knew very well when his walk should be over, and he wanted to go back to his basket now. Ellie realized that the woman with the dogs probably wasn't coming.

Ellie bent down and stroked Angel's pet. "I'm sorry, Ferdi. Let's go back then."

It was such a shame. She'd been so hopeful, but it had come to nothing. Maybe the woman would be there with her dogs another day, and she could try talking to her then. Apart from that, Ellie knew that Francesca would expect her to spend no more work time on Charlie Daniels. Ellie didn't want to admit it, but it was time to move on to the next name on her list.

7
Francesca takes control

Ellie went back to the office feeling rather miserable. She had been so hopeful that she was going to be able to boast about her triumph to everyone, but it had all come to nothing. She tried to tell herself that it didn't matter, but it mattered to *her*. It had been her own project, and it hadn't worked. Then she remembered the email she had sent to the blogger and quickened her pace. Perhaps all wasn't lost after all? Thinking about the possibility that she might have a helpful message from the blogger kept Ellie going until she got back to the office. She changed her shoes, and took Ferdinand back to Angel's office, where he sank down into his basket with a tired but happy sigh and buried his nose under his tail.

Ellie hung up the lead and made her way back to her desk. Piano looked up as she passed, and caught her eye.

"What a shame there were only two of these," she said, pushing a card towards her. "And that Angel gave one to me."

Ellie paused and looked at the card. It was an invitation to a glittering gala charity concert, which no doubt Piano was going to cover for the magazine with Joe Eagle, *Heart*'s photographer. She shrugged. Piano was obviously trying to make her envious. Ellie *did* feel envious, but she wasn't about to show it. However, she couldn't think of anything clever to say, so instead of replying, she simply made her way to her desk and sat down.

Francesca was at her desk too, typing something with great concentration. But she paused to speak to Ellie. "Thanks for getting that packet of inserts for my organizer."

"That's okay," said Ellie. "You're welcome."

Ellie opened her laptop with her fingers and toes crossed for a reply from the blogger. She was sure that if he had made contact she'd feel a million times better. *Please let him have replied,* she thought to herself. *I couldn't bear it if he hasn't.* She told herself that he might be at work and not get the message until the evening, but it didn't change how she felt. She was sure that a bit of success would make her feel better.

She checked her inbox with her heart in her mouth. There was a message. THERE WAS A MESSAGE!

Ellie couldn't believe it. Her spirits soared as, with shaking fingers, she clicked to open it. She read it, and then she read it again. Then her heart sank lower than it had all day. She couldn't help it, even if Piano did notice. She buried her head in her hands and let out a long, discouraged sigh.

For few minutes she sat there, feeling terrible. Then she felt a hand on her shoulder, and Francesca's voice, quietly in her ear. "What's the matter, Ellie? Has something happened? Is it something I can help with?"

Francesca's kindness made Ellie feel like crying, so she couldn't reply straight away.

"Have you had bad news from home?"

Poor Francesca sounded very concerned. Ellie tried to reassure her. She looked up and gave a lopsided smile. "No it's not anything about home," she said.

Francesca frowned. "Well you can't sit here, moping into your computer," she said not unkindly. "Let's go into the boardroom. No one will disturb us there, and you can tell me all about it. All right?"

Ellie nodded. She got to her feet and stumbled towards the exit. She could hear Francesca explaining to Piano that she, Ellie, wasn't well. She felt a fraud, but grateful to

Francesca. In the lobby, Francesca paused to fill a cup with water from the cooler. Then she led the way to the boardroom.

"Now. What's so terrible about my office that it almost reduces you to tears? Has Piano been more sharp than usual? I think you deal with her very well as a rule."

"It's not just Piano getting to me," said Ellie, blowing her nose and then accepting the water. "It's failing with Charlie Daniels too." *I'm sad about Sophie and Flynn as well,* she realized, *everything has added together to make me feel miserable, but I can't say that.*

Ellie explained about finding the blog, and connecting the dogs' names with the ones in the park. "I was so sure I was going to get an address, or at least a phone number," she said. "It was really exciting! But then they didn't come today, and when I got back to find that my email to the blogger had bounced back, labelled 'undeliverable'..." She sighed.

"I just got upset. Sorry."

"Well, never mind," said Francesca. "These things happen. The chances are it's not a live email address if the blog was four years old. Actually," she looked thoughtfully at Ellie, "I think you did remarkably well, considering how little you had to go on. Rather than be sad about it, you should congratulate yourself."

"Really?"

"Of course! A lot of detective work comes to nothing, but when something does come right you know it's all been worth it. You might not have got hold of your man, but you've shown me what you can do. I'm genuinely impressed."

"Well..." Ellie downed the rest of her water and sniffed. "I did enjoy doing it. I'm sorry I got upset. That was stupid."

"Don't worry about it. People who care a lot about what they're doing *can* get upset when it doesn't work out."

Ellie swallowed the lump that had been in her throat. "It's not very professional though."

Francesca smiled. "Maybe not, but that will come. You're young enough to learn in time to hide your feelings a bit more when you need to. But you shouldn't ever be ashamed of having strong feelings. Feelings are honest, and real."

Ellie took a deep breath and gave Francesca a proper smile. "Thanks, Francesca. I know you're really busy, and..."

"Nonsense. It's part of my job, to look after my staff. Look." She paused. "Why don't you go and splash some cool water on your face, repair your make-up and then come back into the office...unless you'd rather I sent you home?"

"No, it's fine," said Ellie quickly.

A few minutes later, Ellie was at her desk again, trying to look as if nothing had happened.

"Would you like a cup of tea?" asked

Francesca. "I'm sure Piano will go and make you one."

"Yes please," said Ellie.

"How do you like it?" asked Piano, immediately pushing back her chair and getting up.

"Milk and one sugar, thanks," said Ellie.

Piano stalked towards the door and Ellie bit back a smile. Of all the things that could have happened to cheer her up, this had to be the best. Piano, making *her* a cup of tea! She glanced over to Francesca. The Deputy Editor gave her a warm smile, and she had a definite twinkle in her eye. Ellie was as certain as she could be that Francesca had done it deliberately. Piano's behaviour towards Ellie might not warrant a telling-off exactly, but it seemed that Francesca had other ways of keeping her staff in line!

8

Interviews

Over the next few days, Ellie threw herself into contacting as many agents as she could, to arrange interviews for the magazine. To her surprise, Kurt Draagan's agent replied very quickly, to say that the star was in London at the moment, and would be pleased to be interviewed straight away. Unfortunately for Ellie, Angel decided she should be the one to do the job. As she was the Editor in Chief, no one could argue about that, although Piano and Debbie were united in thinking that Piano would have been a far better choice.

There was a lot of discussion between Piano and Debbie about what they should wear on the day of Kurt Draagan's interview, just in case he came into the office, although it was almost certain that Angel would interview him at his hotel. Francesca took no part in this. She always remained aloof from such conversations, and Ellie knew that whatever happened, the Deputy Editor would always look cool, sophisticated and way above anything Piano or Debbie could achieve. On the other hand, Piano was great at putting together a really funky look, one that Ellie longed to emulate. But no one, least of all Piano, asked Ellie what she thought.

Ellie was just crossing off the name of a soap star who wasn't going to be available for an interview, when Francesca called her over.

"You remember that visit you made to Jacob Frou last Easter?"

"Do I!" Ellie beamed. She had got on really well with the elderly shoe designer, and had ended the day on a photo shoot, modelling his shoes with Zone One. He might be old, but his designs were seriously cool. She would *never* forget that day, especially as Monsieur Jacob had given her a pair of his shoes as a thank you for modelling for him.

Francesca smiled. "Well I have another designer I'd like you to go and see."

Ellie beamed. "Great! Who is it?"

"A new young designer called Adam Calwell. Angel wants to have a series of articles about the designers who drive the fashion industry. If we're going to look at up-and-coming stars, this guy definitely seems to be one of them. So would you like to interview him?"

Ellie's face lit up. "I'd love to!"

"Okay, give him a ring then," said Francesca. "Angel won't want a huge article, just a brief biography really, with some bits and pieces about how he works, what it's like in his workshop, that sort of thing. And we'll have pictures of some of his designs. It could be the first of a great series for the magazine."

Ellie got onto it straight away. She found Adam Calwell's number in the office database and keyed it in. Almost at once a woman picked up the phone and Ellie explained about the interview.

"I'm sure he'll be delighted to be interviewed," she said. "He's not here at the moment. I'm Julie, his assistant. Hang on. I'll just look in his diary."

There was only one day when Adam was available that week, and Ellie took the offered time straight away. "I was afraid he wouldn't be able to see anyone until the autumn," said Ellie. "And then I would have been back at school. But this is perfect. Thanks so much."

"I'll get back to you if he doesn't want to do it," said Julie. "But I'm sure he'll go for it, especially as it's *Heart* magazine. Your readers are just the right age for his designs."

Ellie put the date in her phone diary and hung up, feeling very pleased with herself. But

Piano must have overheard her conversation. "Don't you like Kurt Draagan?" she enquired with a smirk on her face.

"Of course I do!" said Ellie. "Why?"

"No reason," said Piano. "I just wondered why you were making appointments for the day he's going to be interviewed."

Ellie reminded herself that he was fairly unlikely to come into the office, but she couldn't help looking a bit crestfallen, knowing that he might. Piano, being the sort of person who took pleasure in others' misfortunes, looked almost pleased. "What a shame you'll miss him," she said insincerely, before sashaying back to her desk. "It looks as if he's definitely coming here for Joe to take some pictures."

Ellie could have thumped her desk with frustration. She couldn't ring to rearrange the meeting with Adam Calwell because she knew there wasn't another day he could do. She would just have to resign herself to not seeing her heart-throb and concentrate on enjoying meeting the new designer. *Damn! In fact mega damn.*

At lunchtime she went down to see Sophie.

"I'm sure Flynn thinks I'm stupid not to push myself," Sophie said to Ellie over a shared sandwich. "But at least he's not nagging me about it any more."

Ellie had wondered about telling Sophie that she'd seen Flynn chatting to Debbie, but in the end she didn't feel she could. Maybe he'd just been indulging in a bit of harmless flirting. After all, she hadn't actually overheard anything he'd said. And Ellie didn't want to do anything to make Sophie's relationship with him any more difficult.

In the afternoon, Ellie took Ferdinand for his usual walk. Once again there was no sign of the little dogs with their silver book tags.

"Sorry, Ferdi," said Ellie. "They don't seem to be coming here at the moment."

Back in the office afterwards Debbie seemed a bit grumpy, and Piano was sitting at her desk, concentrating hard on something with a face like thunder.

"What's happened?" Ellie asked Debbie, picking up Ferdinand to give him a last stroke before she returned him to his mistress.

"Angel Makepiece really gets up my nose sometimes," said Debbie in a low voice. There was no sign of the Editor, but it would never do for her to hear such comments from her staff.

"Why's that?" said Ellie.

"She's only changed her mind about Kurt! She's announced that she thinks pictures in his hotel would look better. I'm sure she gets us all excited on purpose, just so she can let us down."

Ellie thought Angel had much more important things to think about than irritating her staff, but she didn't like to say so. "Maybe he doesn't want to come out of his hotel in case he's mobbed by his fans," she said, thinking of all the effort Piano and Debbie had been going to make in the hope that he would notice them. "I expect he gets loads of girls throwing themselves at him, so maybe he wants to avoid that."

"I think she just wants him all for herself," said Debbie, looking thoroughly fed up.

Ellie really didn't want to turn into another version of Piano, but she couldn't resist making some sort of comment as she went past her desk. "I'm so sorry you won't get a chance to see Kurt Draagan," she said sweetly. Piano pretended that she hadn't heard. But when Ellie got back to her desk a rude message appeared on her laptop. It didn't say it came from Piano, but Ellie was as sure as she could be that it had. Ellie deleted it with a smile.

9
Sunshine and rain

On the morning of the interview with Adam Calwell, Ellie wore her Jacob Frou shoes. She was immensely proud of them. They were called the Pirate because they hinted at pirate boots without looking exactly like them. They were lined in the softest red leather, and fastened with a gold coin. What's more, they held her feet as if they were precious objects. They were the only designer items she actually owned. To Ellie the shoes felt so comfortable, it was like walking on clouds, yet at the same time, they always made her want to stamp her feet on echoey wooden floors and dance about with wild abandon.

At the moment she was doing none of these things. She was sitting quietly on a bus, with her notebook on her knees, revising the questions she was going to ask the fashion designer, and hoping that the shoes she was wearing would help him to take her seriously as something of a fashionista. From the bit of research she'd done she knew that his mission statement was to get girls to love dresses. It would be interesting to hear how he intended to do that!

The sun had been shining when she'd set out from home, but now, to her dismay, the sky was clouding over, and it looked like rain. *Oh no! Don't rain. Please don't rain just yet*, she thought. But in no time the bus was driving through a torrential downpour. Ellie was cursing herself for not bringing a coat or umbrella, when the rain suddenly stopped and the sun came out again. Ellie hopped off the bus in high spirits, carefully avoiding the puddles as she headed towards the designer's workshop. She'd almost got there when it happened. A lorry went past, sending a whoosh of water over the pavement where she was walking. It was impossible for her to avoid it, and she was instantly drenched from the knees down in horrible, dirty water.

Ellie rang the doorbell feeling really upset.

Julie let her in. "Adam's looking forward to meeting you," she said, drawing Ellie into the large, light workshop. "But what's the matter?"

"I got splashed by a lorry just before I got to you," said Ellie. "So I'm sorry, but my feet are rather wet."

Julie glanced at the rather sorry-looking Pirates on Ellie's feet and gasped. "What amazing shoes! They're fantastic. But we must clean them up for you. I don't know much about shoes, but I do know that it's very important to dry leather out slowly. Maybe we ought to just clean them off, and leave it at that. Hang on. I'll fetch you a towel for your legs too." Julie stopped chattering and disappeared, leaving Ellie at the door.

"Hi. I thought I heard someone. Come in. You must be Ellie." Adam Calwell was a tall, good-looking man with a closely clipped beard and collar-length, dark hair. He seemed rather amused.

Ellie paused in taking off the Pirates and shook his hand. She had been so determined to look and sound professional, and here she was, caught taking her shoes off and with her skirt and legs splattered with dirty water. It was *so* embarrassing. "I'm sorry," she apologized. "I got splashed, just outside."

"Don't worry," he said. "What was Julie thinking, leaving you here? The workshop is all floorboards, no carpet to ruin... Hang on, are those Jacob Frous?"

"Um..." Ellie pulled the second Pirate off

and straightened up. "Yes, they are. They're called the..."

"Pirate. I know. My goodness, Ellie. They must pay well at *Heart* magazine!"

He was teasing her, but he was so nice she didn't mind, and soon they were chatting like old friends. It seemed that Jacob Frou was a bit of a hero to Adam. He sounded distinctly jealous when Ellie explained how she'd modelled the shoes for Monsieur Frou at a photo shoot before he'd given her the pair she was wearing today.

"I wish he made shoes for men," Adam said as Julie came back with a towel for Ellie. "I bet they'd be fun to wear. Get some of that white paper to pack in the shoes," he added to Julie. "It'll help draw the moisture out. Hopefully they won't feel too wet when you have to put them back on."

"Thank you," said Ellie. She no longer felt embarrassed at talking to Adam in her bare feet, especially now they were sitting in comfortable chairs where there was a soft rug she could dig her toes into.

"So why do you want girls to love dresses?" she asked, notebook at the ready.

"I just think they have so much potential," he told her. "The cut, the length, you can do so much with them. But I try to style all my dresses so that they're easy to wear. And with my designs I hope you can just throw on one of my dresses and accessorize it in your own way." He leaped to his feet and went over to a desk. He came back with some large drawings. "I'm very excited about these," he said. "You know the singer Maia Tonkin?"

"Yes," said Ellie. "She's great."

"Isn't she?" said Adam. "And what's more she's filming her next music video at the Boat Show...*and* she's going to be wearing three of these designs!"

"Wow!" Ellie was seriously impressed. No

wonder Adam seemed so pleased. She scribbled down all the information, but Adam had jumped up from his seat again, and gone back to the desk.

"Here! I've got some extra tickets to the Boat Show, and I don't need them all. Why don't you go along? Maybe you could report on how cool Maia looked in my dresses?"

Adam looked so earnest Ellie had to laugh. "I'll see what my editor says," she said. "But it does sound a good idea. Thank you very much!"

Ellie put the tickets into her bag feeling quite excited. She hoped Francesca would let her go. It had to be a glamorous event, if Maia Tonkin was going to be filming there.

On the way back to the office, Ellie wondered how Angel had got on with her interview. No doubt she had managed to avoid getting drenched by a dirty puddle when she had gone off to meet the dreamy young actor who had taken the film world by storm with his most recent movie. Yes, of course it would have been wonderful if Ellie could have been in on that interview, but she had liked Adam Calwell a lot. Still...Kurt Draagan...Ellie drifted off into a daydream where she and Kurt met in the hotel and hit it off at once. His agent would be ringing up to tell him he had another appointment... but Kurt would only have eyes for Ellie... They'd go out for dinner, and it would be like being in one of his films. He'd gaze at her with his wonderful dark, smoky eyes, and tell her she was everything to him. He'd whisk her off to his country retreat. They'd travel in his luxury custom-built sports car...

Ellie came back to earth when the lady sitting next to her started rummaging in her carrier bag, and poked her in the ribs with her elbow. "Sorry, love. Just looking for my keys."

"That's okay."

The number twenty-seven bus wasn't exactly

like a custom-built sports car, but never mind, the daydream had been good, and Ellie reminded herself that out of all the thousands of Kurt Draagan fans, she was more likely than most to wangle a meeting with him one day. After all, she'd already met Al from Zone One, and he was her favourite singer of all time! Being a journalist for *Heart* did mean she was likely to meet cool and interesting people more often than the rest of her friends.

Back in the office, Ellie started to put her notes in order, ready to show Francesca. She was pleased with all the information she'd gathered, but knew that there wouldn't be room for a big article. Maybe if Francesca looked over what she'd got and gave her some clues about what to use, Ellie might be in with a chance of seeing her own words appear in the magazine, alongside pictures of Adam Calwell and his designs.

It was exciting thinking that her work might

be used, but now it was lunchtime, Ellie had something else on her mind. She wanted to go and see how Sophie was. Hopefully there would be time for a bit of a chat over their sandwiches. Ellie emailed her typed-up notes for Francesca to look at and closed her laptop. Time to go and find Sophie.

Down in the basement, Ellie entered the post room hesitantly. She wanted to catch up with Sophie, but she still felt awkward about finding her and Flynn together. She didn't want to interrupt a blazing row...or them making up. But Sophie was alone, writing on a sticky note.

"Hi, Ellie! Just writing myself a reminder to order more red ink for the franking machine. I utterly refuse to do it before I've eaten my sandwich. I'm starving. There!" She stuck the note onto the wall and smiled. "How's it going? I haven't seen you for a while."

"I've been quite busy."

Ellie told her about her interview that morning, and then they got onto the subject of Charlie Daniels.

"What a shame!" said Sophie when Ellie told her about the trail going cold.

"But I didn't come down to talk about me," said Ellie uncomfortably. "How are things with you?"

"Okay," said Sophie. "Flynn and I haven't exactly made up, but he's not ranting about me and my wasted opportunities any more, so it could be worse."

"Well," said Ellie, having a sudden thought, "how about doing something with me to take your mind off him for a bit? Adam Calwell gave me two tickets for the Boat Show, so I could see Maia Tonkin wearing his designs. I was going to ask Francesca if I could go. I don't actually *need* to for the article. But it would be fun, don't you think?"

"I've never been to a boat show before," said Sophie thoughtfully.

"Neither have I!" said Ellie. "And apparently they have a load of boats floating in the exhibition centre. Indoors! And they're quite big ones, not little dinghies. It sounds fantastic. I just fancied a look, but it doesn't matter. I can go by myself..." Her voice trailed off.

"It does sound fun," said Sophie. "Rocking about in a boat indoors. Crazy! And it *is* just around the corner from here. Okay!" She smiled. "I'm up for it as long as you promise not to mention Flynn or my pots."

Ellie laughed. "Done!"

10
At the Boat Show

Francesca thought it was a good idea for Ellie to go and watch the music video being filmed.

"You might get another article out of it," she said. "And at the very least it'll be an interesting experience for you. And it's perfect that Sophie is going to go with you, otherwise I might be a bit concerned. But you'll be fine with her."

The day of the video filming both Ellie and Sophie felt as if they were escaping, as they left the building soon after three o'clock. There was only one slight downer. Ellie had Ferdinand in tow. Angel had spotted Ellie changing her shoes in the lobby as she came back from a meeting.

"Are you coming in or going out?" she had said, pausing at the door.

"Um…going out," said Ellie.

"Well you seem to have forgotten my dog," said Angel. "Hurry up and fetch him. I've got someone coming in this afternoon who doesn't like dogs, so don't bring him back before five."

"What could I do?" said Ellie to Sophie as they walked down the street. "I couldn't say no. Not to Angel. I thought Piano was going to take him out for his walk, but of course she'd disappeared somewhere, just at that moment."

"That sounds typical Piano behaviour," Sophie laughed. "But it doesn't matter. He's no trouble, is he? And he seems quite pleased to be out."

"That's true."

In fact Ferdinand was looking very happy indeed. Unusually he was being taken in the opposite direction to the park; it was a new adventure for him and he totally perked up. He trotted along with his head held high, as if he was in a dog show. It made Ellie giggle to see him high-stepping his way along the street.

It didn't take too long to walk to the huge exhibition centre. Unfortunately, at the entrance there was a sign saying **No Animals**. Ellie was crestfallen. "If only Angel hadn't caught me!" she said, but Sophie yanked her past the entrance.

"Don't stop," she muttered. "Come over here."

Ellie joined her at the corner of the building. "What are you doing?" she said. "Look, I can't go in, but you can. Here's your ticket. It's so annoying. I'll miss the filming! But it can't be helped. I'll go to the park now. I can't take Ferdinand back yet, Angel would kill me!"

"Don't be such a wimp," said Sophie. "It's getting on towards the end of the day. The people on the door aren't going to be taking much notice. Didn't you say that when you first saw Ferdinand under Angel's arm you thought he was some sort of hairy handbag? Why not carry him round? They'll never notice."

Ellie spluttered with laughter. "We can't do that!" she said. "What if they *did* notice? And don't they check everyone's bags at the door?"

"Well they won't be able to look in this one," said Sophie, starting to laugh too. "Go on. Just give it a try."

They both looked down at Ferdinand, who gazed back at them, wagging his tail. "Well..." Ellie bent down and picked him up, stifling a giggle.

"Tuck him under your arm more," said Sophie, looking at them critically. "His feet are dangling down. That's better." She stood back with her hands on her hips. "That's fi— Oh." Ferdinand had raised his head and licked Ellie's chin.

"It's no good," said Ellie, giggling in spite of her disappointment. "I'd never get away with it."

Sophie looked stubborn. "Yes you will. If—" she took hold of the light raincoat Ellie had put on to come out. "I know! Button him inside your coat. Go on. They'll never notice him then. They'll just think you're a bit plump." Sophie saw Ellie's doubtful expression and laughed.

"What's the worst they're going to do?" she said. "Throw you out, that's all. And if they do I'll go with you. Come on. It'll be a laugh. And what harm can it do? Ferdinand won't disgrace himself will he? He'll be on the lead."

"Well…"

"I'd hold him, but he knows you better than me." Sophie shook Ellie's arm. "Go on. Say yes. I'll link arms with you, and I'll hand in the tickets. You said you wanted to take my mind off my problems. Well come on then!"

Ellie couldn't help laughing, even though she was scared at the idea of being caught by the ticket collectors. "I thought you were sensible!" she said.

"I am usually," said Sophie. "And I wouldn't have suggested bringing Ferdinand just so we could try this trick...but we're here now, and we have him with us...and it seems a shame to just give up. Isn't tomorrow the last day?"

Ellie looked at the huge sign outside the exhibition hall. "Yes. But the filming is today."

"Well then. Come on. If it doesn't work I won't mind. We can go to the park instead, and I'll buy you an ice cream...unless it rains, in which case we'll have to go to a café and leave Ferdinand tied up outside."

"I couldn't do that! Angel would have a *fit*. Imagine if he got stolen! She'd never forgive me." Ellie gave him an awkward stroke through her coat. "Okay then. Let's try it. But I hope my mum never gets to hear about this. She'd go almost as ballistic as Angel."

Sophie grinned. "I won't tell her if you don't. Right. Tuck Ferdi in, and I'll do your coat up to hide him."

They were both giggling uncontrollably by the time Ferdinand was properly buttoned inside Ellie's coat. "You look pregnant," said Sophie, as she stood back to look at Ellie.

"Well thanks a bunch!" said Ellie, trying to sound affronted and failing. "Come on. If we're going to do this we ought to do it now. He's not going to stay still for very long."

"All right. Let's go." Sophie checked that Ferdinand's nose was well out of sight and the two girls hurried to the entrance. Sophie was right, the ticket collectors weren't very interested in them. There were two of them, having a chat. They took the complimentary tickets, looked briefly into Sophie's bag and waved the girls through the security gates, and continued their conversation. In a matter of moments Ellie, Sophie and Ferdinand were all inside, and the girls were trying not to collapse with laughter.

"Where's this pretend harbour with real

water and boats then?" said Sophie, trying to sober up a bit.

"I don't know," said Ellie. "The harbour is where the filming will be, but here it's all just trade stands."

In fact, it was all trade stands as far as they could see, rows and rows of them, all showing anything and everything that a sailor could possibly want. Some of the stands looked unbelievably boring, with lots of gadgets that meant nothing to Ellie or Sophie. But others were more promising. There was a boot stand that had a huge array of colourful sailing boots and shoes.

"There are boots with built-in trousers!" said Ellie with a squeal. "Look! They've got braces to hold them up."

"Haven't you ever seen those before?" said Sophie.

Ellie shook her head. "Look at those sunglasses!" she said. "They are really cool."

"Steady," said Sophie, pulling Ellie's collar closer around her neck. "Ferdi's nose is peeping out."

"I don't blame him," said Ellie. "I expect there are lots of new smells for him. And it's hot in here. Carrying him in my coat is like holding a hot water bottle."

"Oh look!" said Sophie. "I've always wanted to have a go on one of these."

She hurried to a nearby stand that had a board rigged up so that you could try windsurfing on dry land. Ellie followed more slowly. She was getting very hot, and she suspected Ferdinand was too, by the way she could feel him panting. She opened her collar again and he pushed his little black nose out under her chin. He seemed happy enough, in spite of being hot. She could feel his tail trying to wag against her stomach.

Sophie was talking to the man in charge of the windsurfer, and now he seemed to be urging her to have a go. Ellie groaned. The show certainly seemed to be cheering Sophie up, but Ellie wished there was somewhere to sit down while Sophie tried the windsurfer. Ferdinand might be small, but he felt increasingly heavy as the minutes passed. And Ellie was getting hotter and hotter.

To distract herself from thinking about how uncomfortable she was, Ellie started walking slowly past some of the other stands in the same row as the windsurfer. She didn't want to lose Sophie, but she couldn't stand still any longer. Besides, she really ought to go and find the set for the video filming, or she'd miss seeing Maia Tonkin in Adam's dresses. She wandered down one side of the row, passing innumerable stands selling yacht insurance, residential sailing courses and security items for boats. They were all totally boring. She got to the end and turned round to come back. The stands on the other side were no better. There were estate agents offering apartments and houses with mooring facilities, lots of navigation equipment that meant nothing to Ellie, and more sailing courses.

Then, out of the corner of her eye, Ellie noticed something that she recognized. To begin with, she wasn't quite sure what it was that had caught her eye. It was something about the way the little stand was laid out. And yet it looked much like lots of others. There was a table, with brochures advertising moorings for sale in an "alternative" marina. There were a couple of comfy seats, blown-up photographs of the marina pinned to the back wall and a few decorative features to make the stand seem more inviting. At the back, in one corner, was a large floor lamp next to a low table that had a bowl of nuts on it, and in the other corner was a large pot, filled with some dried grasses.

Ellie stared at the pot. Until she'd met Sophie, one pot had looked much like another, but she was sure she recognized this one. Taking note of the number of the stand she hurried back to Sophie, who still hadn't finished her go on the windsurfer. She was flushed and looked to be hugely enjoying herself. She noticed Ellie and waved to her, almost overbalancing as she did so. A couple of minutes later she climbed off the simulator and joined Ellie.

"That was the *most* fun I've had in ages!" she said. "I really must try windsurfing next time I'm at the sea."

"Never mind that," said Ellie impatiently. "Come and look at this!"

"What is it?" said Sophie. "Hang on. Don't go so fast. I'm feeling a bit wobbly now I'm back on dry land."

Ellie shot Sophie a sceptical look and kept going. As soon as she arrived back at the stand she stopped. "You know I promised not to mention the word P.O.T.S.?"

"Yes?" Sophie laughed. "Ha! You just have!"

In reply, Ellie simply pointed to the dried grasses, sitting decoratively at the back of the stand. Sophie looked, and Ellie heard her gasp. "My pot!"

In a couple of seconds she was kneeling on the floor, running her hands over the blue glaze, her face ecstatic. "It *is* mine! I can't believe that it's here. I didn't know that it had been sold!"

"I thought it must be one of yours," said Ellie, feeling very pleased with herself for spotting it.

"The gallery must have sold it for me," said Sophie, looking up. "It's the twin of the one I keep in the post room. Oh, Ellie. I can't believe it!"

A man had appeared from the next-door stand. "Can I help you?" he asked, looking a bit bemused.

Sophie scrambled to her feet, while Ellie hitched Ferdinand to a more comfortable position. "It's just that...this is my pot...I mean, I made this pot," said Sophie. "And I just wondered if you knew who had bought it."

"Oh. Right." The man looked relieved. "I wondered what you were doing. People usually want to see the literature rather than the decorations." He paused. "Actually the pot is Mark Kettle's, he owns the marina. He's just nipped off to get a sandwich. If you wait a few minutes I'm sure he won't be long. I'm just keeping an eye on his stand for him." He looked at Ellie and then back to Sophie. "Perhaps your friend would like to sit down while you wait? She looks tired...can I get you something?" he went on to Ellie. "A drink of water perhaps?"

Ellie would have loved to sit down, but she was sure that if she did she'd start giggling again, and Ferdinand would start wriggling. In fact, he was beginning to wriggle now. She clasped her hands more firmly around her bulging raincoat, hugging him to her and shook her head. "It's okay, thanks," she said to the man, managing not to dissolve into hysterics. "I think I'll go and find the harbour, while Sophie waits. Do you know where it is? There's some filming going on there."

"Don't you have a map of the show?" He offered his. "Along there, turn right, and right again. You can't miss it. Just head for the masts." He pointed up and Ellie saw a cluster of masts, swaying slightly above the stands. Of course! She should have thought to look up before. "Are you sure you're all right?" he asked Ellie.

"I'm fine," she said quickly. "I'll try and find Maia Tonkin," she said to Sophie. "Text me when you're ready."

"Are you sure?"

"Of course!" Ellie practically ran from the stand and the helpful man, hitching Ferdinand higher as she did so. The poor man had obviously thought she was expecting a baby!

He had been so kind. She would have hated him to think she was laughing at him. She dodged quickly along the way he had shown her. With luck she'd be in time for the filming and maybe she'd find a quiet corner to sit and watch until Sophie turned up.

She kept going, thinking of Sophie's pot, and the boats, and of how lovely it would be to sit down when the unimaginable happened. Suddenly, Ferdinand gave an almighty wriggle. He slid out of her arms and under the coat, ending up sprawled on the floor by her feet. But before she could grab him he had gone, galloping gleefully away, trailing his lead behind him.

11
Come back, Ferdinand!

Ellie had felt Ferdinand sliding, and done her best to hold him, but with her raincoat buttoned over him it was impossible. Before she could grab his lead, he'd scampered off. Ellie chased after him; however, it was a lot busier in this part of the exhibition hall, and he dodged easily between people's legs, while Ellie had to keep saying "Excuse me" and trying to push past as quickly as possible without annoying anyone too much.

Ellie's heart felt as if it was trying to leap out of her ribcage and into her throat. She was choking with anxiety, and getting so hot she was beginning to fear that she might pass out.

She pushed stubbornly on, desperate not to lose Angel's dog. The thought of going back into the office without him was simply unimaginable. What if he was caught by an official and put in a dog pound? Would she ever find him again? Or what if someone dognapped him? He would be helpless. He wasn't the sort of dog that bit people. He trusted everyone.

Ellie had never been concerned about dognappers before, but then Ferdinand had never been out of her sight before now. Angel tended to hold him under her arm like a handbag; well sometimes dogs got stolen to *make* bags. Ellie was almost sure of it. She'd watched a programme about it years ago, and had had nightmares afterwards. Angel trusted her to take care of her little dog, and now she'd gone and betrayed that trust.

Ellie wormed her way between two large men wearing sailing caps and caught a sudden glimpse of tall masts waving at her. Boats were sitting on the water, and seagulls were screaming overhead. The sun seemed to be burning down and making her feel dizzy, which was odd, because she knew she was indoors. She saw the harbour wall, with a row of pastel-painted houses on the far side. Near to her there was a café, with busy, outside tables bathed in the sunshine. It all seemed unreal. There was something wrong with the picture, but she couldn't work out what it was. Then she caught a glimpse of a little dog scampering along the harbourside. She wanted to call out, but her head was spinning, and the waving masts, mewing seagulls and the people at the café tables were becoming blurred. All at once, Ellie felt her legs go from under her and she passed out.

She could only have been out for a few seconds, because when she came to, a woman was still lowering her to the ground, while a couple of waiters kept the crowd away to give her some space and air.

Ellie tried to sit up, but the woman pushed her back again. "Don't struggle," she said in a kind voice. "I'm a doctor. It's lucky I was nearby. I could see you weren't well, and I was afraid you were going to hit your head, but between me and another lady we managed to catch you."

"I'm all right," said Ellie. "I just got too hot."

The doctor helped her off with her coat and someone brought a drink of cool water. The doctor allowed her to take a few sips of the water while she kept an eye on her. After a few more minutes, Ellie was allowed to get up and sit on a chair. All the time she was fretting about Ferdinand, but didn't want to admit that she'd brought a dog into the exhibition hall.

"Thank you so much for helping me," she said after a few more precious minutes had passed. "I feel fine now."

"Well, I don't think you ought to be in a hurry to move," said the doctor. "Just sit here for a bit longer and enjoy the view."

Ellie looked out over the harbour and saw the row of houses again; except now she could see that there weren't any houses at all. The view was actually a painted backdrop to the little artificial harbour that had been made for the Boat Show. The sun was just some bright white lights shining down, and the seagull sounds were obviously recordings. She could see now that most of the harbour was an illusion. There was water, but it had to be in a huge sunken tank in the floor, and there were a few boats tied up to a mock-up of a harbour wall. The ground under Ellie's feet looked like paving stones, but now she realized it was some sort of artificial flooring, with a few tubs of real flowers near the harbour wall to reinforce the illusion. The effect was lovely, but Ellie was worrying about the glimpse she thought she'd had of Ferdinand, just before she passed out. Had it really been him, or had she imagined it? And what on earth was she going to do about finding him? He could be anywhere by now.

She had to get hold of Sophie. She didn't want to interrupt whatever she was doing, but this was an emergency. Ellie pulled out her phone and texted. *I'm at the Harbour Lights café. Are you going to be long?*

In a couple of minutes a text came back. *All finished here. I owe you!!!! Be with you in a few minutes.*

Ellie sighed with relief. Sophie would know what to do. And the kindly doctor would be much more likely to let her patient go if she had someone with her. "My friend is on her way," she said to the doctor. "Thank you so much for looking after me, but I'll be fine now. I don't usually make a habit of fainting."

The doctor smiled down at her. "That's good. Yes, I'm sure you'll be fine. But if you do start getting fainting fits do go and get a check-up.

I expect you're right though. It is pretty hot and airless in here, and you were much too hot in that coat."

"I know," said Ellie. "It was silly of me to keep it on." She saw Sophie making her way towards her and waved. "Here's my friend. Thanks again. I really appreciate it."

"I'll leave you to it then." The doctor waited until Sophie arrived and then gave them both a friendly wave. "Bye then. Enjoy the rest of your day. Just take it steady from now on."

Sophie plonked herself down in the chair next to Ellie and picked up the menu. "Sorry I was so long, but I have just had the most unbelievably fantastic time! You won't believe this...I actually met Mark Kettle! And he wants another of my pots. I owe you big time, Ellie... Ellie? What's the matter?"

Ellie could feel tears trickling down her face and brushed them away with her hands. "I've lost Ferdinand."

Sophie gasped. "Oh, Ellie! How stupid of me. You're not wearing your coat any more, and I never even noticed. What happened? Where were you? How long ago?"

The tears kept coming, and there was nothing Ellie could do about it.

"Come on, Ellie," said Sophie, putting her arm around her friend. "We'll find him. This is all my stupid fault. I should never have encouraged you to smuggle him in. Let's think. There must be a tannoy system. We can get an announcement put out, to alert people to look for him."

Ellie tried not to hiccup. "But he's...not supposed to *be* here!"

"You let me worry about that. But...where did you lose him? We could have a look ourselves first. If we split up we might come across him. If not we'll get an announcement made. It'll be okay. You'll see."

Sophie was sounding confident, but she

looked very worried, and Ellie was sure she was being upbeat to cheer her up. In this crowd, the chance of finding a little dog wasn't great.

Ellie wiped her tears away again and tried to think. "I might have caught a glimpse of him running along over there," she said, pointing towards the harbour wall, where the boats were tied up. There were loads of people there, admiring the boats, so it was difficult to see anything much.

"Did you?" Sophie sounded doubtful. "Well why don't we split up. You go that way, I'll go this way and we'll meet back here in say fifteen minutes?"

"Okay."

They both got to their feet and Sophie put the menu back on the table. "When we find him I'll buy you the biggest cake in the café!" she said with an effort to be light-hearted. She looked at Ellie, concerned. "Are you all right? You look very pale."

"I'm fine," said Ellie, not wanting to hold things up even more by explaining about her fainting fit. "See you in quarter of an hour."

Sophie was soon swallowed up by the crowd and Ellie headed for the harbour wall, where she thought she'd last seen Ferdinand. He was used to spending a lot of time sitting quietly in his basket in the office. Did that mean he'd want to find a quiet place by now, or would he still be galloping along, enjoying his freedom? In one way it was good that he was trailing his lead. Anyone would be able to stand on it to catch him, but what if the lead got caught up on something and got all tangled up? His little legs were so thin: Ellie couldn't bear to think of him being hurt.

She pushed her way through the throng of people, trying to keep an eye on the ground. It was extremely difficult, and she could see almost no distance ahead. She'd have to practically trip over him before she could see him.

She worked her way past the boats floating on the water. There were several little dinghies, and two larger boats. One was a cabin cruiser, which looked very cool. The other was shaped rather like a fishing boat, but it didn't have any fishing gear on its spacious deck, and was obviously meant for leisure. Ellie looked down into a small dinghy and shuddered. She really *didn't* want to contemplate the possibility that Ferdinand might have fallen off the harbour wall.

She searched as far round the harbour as she could – though the painted row of houses was cordoned off – and worked her way back towards the café. There was a whole collection of eateries near the harbour, and it took her some time to peer under every table and chair. Luckily, at this time in the afternoon not too many people were sitting at the tables. Earlier in the day the cafés and bars would have been heaving. Eventually, she made it back to the

Harbour Lights café and flopped into a nearby seat. It was no use. She had no idea where Ferdinand was. They would have to own up and hope that *someone* had seen him somewhere in the exhibition.

After a few minutes more Sophie arrived back. She shook her head. "It's nothing like so crowded away from this area, but I can't see any sign of him." She put her hands on her hips and gazed around. "Look. There's a huge crush over by those painted houses. That must be where they're filming Maia Tonkin's video. They've got lights, and everything."

"Oh yes," said Ellie dully. "Maia Tonkin. I was supposed to be watching that, wasn't I?" She peered over towards the harbour, but it was impossible to see anything. Ellie wondered if she ought to see if she could push her way through the crowd, but with Ferdinand lost she didn't care about being a journalist any more. All she wanted was to have the little dog safely back.

"I asked at a few stands," said Sophie, trying to be helpful. "I gave them my number and they said they'd text if they saw him." She sighed. "Where *has* he got to?"

Ellie leaned her elbows on the table. "We've got to tell someone official. What if he's tangled up in his lead? What if he's hurt? Where do we go to get an announcement made?"

Sophie was taking a last look around. "You're right. There must be a help desk somewhere. I'll ask one of the staff in he— Oh, Ellie, look!"

Ellie looked in the direction Sophie was pointing, but could see nothing.

"Over there! I saw him. He was carrying something!"

Ellie stood up to see better, and then, in the gap between a young couple strolling past and an elderly gentleman, she caught a glimpse of a small dog, trotting purposefully along, carrying what looked like a large bone in his mouth. "Ferdi! Here!" Ellie was off like a hare, weaving between people as fast as she could, the brief sight of Ferdinand etched onto her brain. It was so frustrating. One quick sighting, and he was obscured by people again, people who were in no hurry to get out of her way. "Ferdi!"

Another sighting came as she pushed unapologetically past a gaggle of middle-aged women. "Ferdi!" But it was no use. The little dog hadn't heard her. And then, to her dismay he started to run, put on a spurt, and disappeared again by the gangplank of the cabin cruiser.

Cornered

Ellie followed as best as she could. When she reached the spot where she'd last seen Ferdinand she stood still, casting about for a clue.

"Did you see a little dog here a moment ago?" she asked a man who was reading a leaflet he'd taken from a nearby table. He shook his head. Ellie was trembling. She was afraid she might cry again, and told herself sternly not to. Ferdinand was okay. He didn't look at all hurt, and he was somewhere nearby. All she had to do was find him. Though where he'd got that bone from she dreaded to think. Maybe he'd stolen it from one of the kitchens attached to the cafés.

Sophie caught up with Ellie and grabbed her arm. "Have you lost him again?"

"Yes. He was running along just here, but then I couldn't see which way he went. It was a bone he was carrying!"

A girl about Sophie's age, who was nearby, looking at the boats, swivelled round to speak to Ellie. "Are you talking about that dog that just ran past?"

Ellie and Sophie looked at her eagerly. "Yes!" said Ellie. "Did you see him?"

The girl laughed. "I certainly did. He was so cute, trotting along with a bone in his mouth. Is he yours?"

"Yes," said Ellie to avoid time-wasting explanations. "Which way did he go?"

"That's easy," said the girl, looking even more amused. "He was trotting past the boats when something attracted his attention. He seemed to suddenly change his mind and darted up the gangplank."

"Which gangplank?" said Sophie, looking at both the large vessels that were tied up to the harbour wall.

The girl pointed at the one shaped like a fishing boat. "He went on that one," she said. "And I'm not totally sure, but I don't think he's come back off it yet."

"We've got him!" said Sophie gleefully.

They made their way swiftly to the boat's gangplank, but were pulled up short by a slim gate that barred their way. Ellie could see that it would have been easy enough for Ferdinand to slip between the bars, but for them it would be impossible. To make matters worse, a notice had been hung over the gate. *NO ENTRY*, it said in red letters. There didn't seem to be anyone in charge to ask for help. Ellie rattled the gate in frustration.

"I thought you were supposed to be allowed on these boats," she said. "People are going on and off the other one."

163

"Don't worry," said Sophie, putting a restraining hand on Ellie's arm. "I'll go and find someone to help us. You stay here and watch in case he comes back off. We've got him cornered now. It's just a matter of time." She disappeared at a jog, and Ellie settled down to wait. She glanced at her watch and got a shock. She had assumed it was about four o'clock, but it was just after five. Angel might be wanting to go home, and she would certainly be wondering where Ellie had got to with her dog!

Ellie looked around for Sophie, but there was no sign of her. This was dreadful. She needed to take Ferdinand back to his mistress now! She rattled the gate again, and then noticed something. The gate wasn't actually locked. She'd thought it was because of the notice, but actually it was simply latched. She could open it, walk through and search the boat for Ferdinand – if no one noticed her, that was. She looked around, but there didn't seem to be anyone in charge. And there was still no sign of Sophie. Quickly, before she could falter, Ellie opened the gate, sidled through and closed it behind her. There was no going back now!

She made her way up the gangplank towards the boat, expecting a shout to come from behind her at any moment, telling her to come back. But the shout never came. In a moment she was at the boat, and she swiftly jumped down off the gangplank and into the wheelhouse at the stern. Although it was securely tied up, when she landed, the boat dipped and rose again with her added weight. She stumbled at the unexpected movement. She'd almost forgotten it was actually floating.

It was a lovely boat. She could imagine sunbathing on the deck, while some handsome film star steered them towards the sunset, but this was no time for daydreaming. She needed to find Ferdinand...and fast! She went down a step, so she could see into the cabin. There he was! But he wasn't alone. Ellie stared at the person he was with. For a few moments she couldn't take it all in, and the person seemed to be having difficulty taking Ellie in too.

"Ferdinand!"

Angel Makepiece's little dog was sitting at the feet of a woman...a woman Ellie recognized. She was holding his collar, and looking at his tag...which was the very thing Ellie had tried to do with *her* dog in the park not so long ago. There was no sign of her little dogs though; Snappit and Beastly must have been left at home, as Ferdinand should have been.

The woman looked at Ellie as if she couldn't quite believe she was there. "You seem to have lost your dog," she said at last. "He caught sight of me and came rushing up the gangplank."

"I expect he recognized you," said Ellie faintly. "Like I did." Relief at finding Ferdinand safe and unharmed jostled with the shock of seeing him with Snappit and Beastly's owner.

"We met at the park," she explained. But it was obvious that the woman had recognized her too.

"I remember," said the woman. "This is your boss's dog, isn't it?"

Ellie nodded. "I work for *Heart*..."

"The magazine," the woman finished for her. "Yes. And I'm sorry I had to rush off that last time. I did feel I was being a bit rude but..."

"I thought it was a bit odd," said Ellie truthfully. "But then I wondered...you see...I think you know Charlie Daniels!" she gabbled before she could stop herself. "And you didn't want me to find out."

Just then someone else appeared through an inner door. It was a boy who looked a bit older than Ellie. He was in time to hear what she'd said and laughed. The woman looked urgently at him, but the same time as she said, "No," he said, "Yes."

The woman looked cross. She turned to the boy. "Don't, Daniel," she said.

"It's all right," he said. "It doesn't matter any more."

Ellie looked from one to the other, but neither of them seemed tempted to elaborate. Finding Ferdinand safe and, bizarrely, with the very woman she'd been hoping to meet in the park, she felt reckless, and didn't care if they thought her rude to pursue the subject.

"I found out that Charlie Daniels used to have two dogs," she told the boy. "They were called Snippit and Snappit."

The boy looked very startled for a moment, then recovered himself and smiled. "And your point is…?" he said.

"Well," said Ellie. "Maybe Snippit died. If so, I'm sorry, but you still have Snappit, don't you? Ferdinand used to play with him and Beastly until…"

The boat rocked again and Ellie wondered if it might be Sophie. But it wasn't her. It was a man, wearing a badge that showed he worked for Replica Boats Inc. He seemed both worried and annoyed.

He looked at the woman. "I do apologize. I know you didn't want to be disturbed. I'll remove this young lady and her dog immediately."

"NO!"

They all stared at Ellie. "I'm sorry," she said to the woman and the boy called Daniel. "I will go in a minute, and I'm sorry about the dog, and disturbing you and everything..." Her voice faltered for a moment and then she went stubbornly on. "I didn't know you were going to be here...but you are...and I've been looking for Charlie Daniels for so long. I've tried the publisher, the agent...trawled through thousands of websites...I went to a bookshop and the library. And I'd wanted to talk to you in the park," she said accusingly to the woman. "But you stopped coming, and so I had to give up. I had worked so hard at it..."

"And you've done so well!" said Daniel. "Really. You have."

The woman put her hand on his sleeve but he shook her off gently. "It's okay, Mum," he said. "Really. It's all right. I don't mind now." He smiled at the man who had offered to remove Ellie. "She can stay," he said, and looked at his mother. "Can't she?" His mother looked exasperated, but then she smiled at her son and nodded slightly.

"What about the dog?"

"I'll take the dog."

Everyone turned to where Sophie was standing in the doorway. She had come on board much more quietly than Ellie or the man, and no one had heard her. "Give him to me, Ellie. I'll take Ferdinand back. After all, I owe you." She looked at the official. "It's my fault he's here, so if you need to escort me off the premises go ahead."

Ellie picked up Ferdinand's lead and handed

him over to Sophie. She smiled at Ellie. "Don't worry," she said. "I won't say a word to anyone...about anything. You've obviously got stuff to do here. I'll see you tomorrow."

"Thanks, Sophie!" Ellie wondered what on earth Sophie would say to Angel. No doubt Ellie would find out later, and it wasn't something she was looking forward to. She hoped Sophie wouldn't get into too much trouble.

When Sophie and the official had gone Ellie stood in the cabin of the boat, wondering what to say next. The woman stood up and went over to close the door. It was suddenly very quiet.

"So," said Daniel with an amused expression on his face. "Tell us exactly what you know, and how you know it, and I'll tell you if you're right."

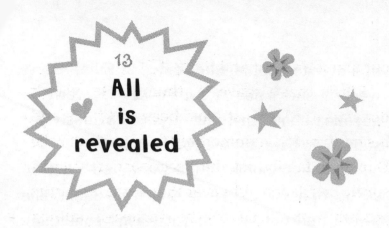

13
All is revealed

"All right," said Ellie. "I'll tell you what I know, but it's not very much."

"Wait a moment," said the woman. "I could really do with a cup of tea. Do sit down if you're staying, and chat to Daniel for a minute. I'm going to put the kettle on. Would you like a cup of tea, or a soft drink? The fridge is quite well equipped I think." Without waiting for an answer she disappeared into the galley, and Ellie looked at Daniel.

He patted the seat next to him. "Sit down. And call me Dan. Mum is the only one who calls me Daniel, and then only when she's cross." He grinned. "Tell me how you found out about Snappit and Snippit."

Ellie's heart gave a thump. He wasn't denying it! She must have been right. He and his mum *did* have something to do with Charlie Daniels's family...at the very least they must surely be friends. Whoever they were, Ellie was getting very close to the reclusive author. Maybe he was even on the boat at this very minute!

"I found a blog," she told Dan, trying hard to sound calm, even though she could feel her excitement rising. "By someone called Matt Budgeon."

Dan looked astonished. "Really? I thought he'd stopped that ages ago."

"It was quite old," she said. "I'd looked through all the newest websites, blogs and articles about Charlie Daniels that I could find, but there was nothing to go on. So I tried starting at the back and working forward instead. There still wasn't much, except for the old blog. I needed to get in touch," she explained, "to ask if he'd let me interview him."

Dan was shaking his head. "Hang on. What made you think Charlie Daniels would let you interview him, when he hasn't *ever* given an interview?"

Ellie blushed. "Well, I want to be a journalist," she explained. "Like my dad was. And I have this sort of part-time job for a magazine...well it's work experience really but..."

"So what do your mum and dad think about you chasing after people for interviews?" It was Dan's mum, carrying a tray with a mug of tea, two glasses of orange juice and a plate of expensive-looking biscuits.

Ellie took a glass of orange. "Thanks. Mum's fine about it. And my dad died just before I was born. He was a war correspondent."

The boy stared at her. "Wow. I mean... sorry."

Ellie found herself smiling at him to make light of his confusion. "It's okay. And I have his notebook, which is really cool."

"So. You read Matt's blog, which is amazing, because we're mates from school, and he didn't do the blog for long. It was just a joke. He was always into computers and the net...and names. In fact Charlie Daniels was his idea. He was so pleased when we decided to go with it – it made his day."

Ellie wondered what Dan meant.

The boy's mum sipped her tea. "So what did Matt Budgeon say that alerted you to us?"

"He was writing about *dogs'* names. He was saying that it was good to have names in pairs, and one pair he mentioned was Snippit and Snappit, who belonged to the 'soon to be famous' Charlie Daniels."

"He said that?" Dan was laughing as he looked at his mum.

His mum offered Ellie a biscuit. "I can fill in

the rest. You saw me and the dogs in the park, heard Snappit's name and put two and two together."

"I'm sorry," said Ellie, nibbling the biscuit, "I didn't want to take pictures, or reveal where he lives, or anything like that. I just hoped he'd let me ask him some questions about his writing and the films."

"And now you're getting your wish," said the boy.

Ellie looked at him. "I am?"

He nodded.

"You mean...he's here? And will talk to me?" Ellie fumbled in her bag for her notebook. "I won't take up much of his time..."

Now Dan *and* his mum were laughing. Ellie felt a bit put out, but the woman soon took pity on her. "You'll have to tell her now, Dan. Or do you want me to?"

"I will." The boy cleared his throat. "You are already talking to Charlie Daniels."

Ellie stared at him, open-mouthed. "You? You're Charlie Daniels?" She probably sounded rude, but she couldn't help it. She hadn't in her wildest dreams imagined that the author would be so young.

"Well, I'm the Daniels part, or Daniel, to be correct as it's my name. The other half is my mum here, Charlotte...better known as Charlie."

"But..." Ellie looked from one to the other. "I thought he was a man."

"That's what we wanted everyone to think," said Charlie. "You see, a couple of years ago, when we got this big advance for the books, Daniel was still at school, working for his A levels. If the papers had got hold of the story, he wouldn't have had any peace."

"The publishers suggested we come up with a pseudonym and Matt's name for us seemed perfect," said Dan. "And it worked really well, but it's not so important to keep the secret now.

I've taken my exams, and I'm going to take a gap year before university, while Mum and I write the next book." He threw his arms wide to include the whole cabin. "And we're going off sailing!"

His enthusiasm was infectious, and Ellie found herself smiling back. "In this boat?"

He nodded. "We've just bought it! It's our first big treat since we started earning so much money. Do you like it?"

"I do," said Ellie, full of admiration.

As they devoured the biscuits, Dan and Charlie explained how it had all happened. How, when Dan's dad had died a few years earlier, Dan had told his mum that he'd help to make enough money for them to live. How it had started more as a way for them to share a hobby, but had ended up as a bit of an obsession, one that turned into the Fanghurst Trilogy that had sold so many copies and was now being turned into three films.

"The thing is," said Charlie thoughtfully, "I'm not sure our publisher will want a teen magazine like *Heart* to be the one to reveal the secret. They are planning a big event this summer. They want to keep the books uppermost in people's minds. It's an ideal time, with the first film being such a hit, and the second one due out soon."

"Well I don't want to spoil their plans," said Ellie wistfully.

"But Ellie did all the sleuthing to find out," said Dan. "It won't be fair if she doesn't get her scoop. At least her magazine ought to be able to reveal who we are at the same time as the publisher."

"It's going to depend on timing," said Charlie. "I expect your magazine is monthly, isn't it?"

Ellie nodded.

"Well, our publisher won't want to risk waiting any longer, now you've uncovered our secret," said Charlie, "in case it gets leaked. I don't know if it would be possible for you to run the story at the same time or not. But I tell you what: Dan, why don't you give *Heart* your first interview? We'll have to do a joint one I expect, pretty quickly, but I don't see why Ellie shouldn't do an interview just with you. You're the one who will interest a magazine like *Heart*. I'll clear it with the publishers. We haven't signed over *all* our decision making for publicity."

"That would be *brilliant!*" said Ellie, hardly able to believe her ears. "It's exactly the sort of thing the readers of *Heart* will love."

"I'll phone our publicist," said Charlie with a smile. "To be honest, although it was good to stay out of the limelight for a while, it's rather a relief to know that we won't have to live a lie for much longer."

"Will you be prepared to have photographs taken as well?" said Ellie hopefully. "You could come into the office for the interview and a photo shoot if you like."

"Why not?" said Dan. "It sounds fun, and now the secret is out there's no point being shy. But look...in case none of this works out...I'll make sure you have a couple of tickets for the premiere of the next film. How about that as a reward for your persistence?"

14
Another surprise

As soon as Ellie had got the contact numbers for Dan and his mum she hurried back to the office. Some of the staff would have left already, but she needed to collect some of her things, and she hoped that she might be able to make sure that Sophie was okay. Had she got into terrible trouble with Angel for bringing Ferdinand back so late? And would Ellie be in trouble too, for not arriving back with him at all?

On top of that, if Francesca was there, Ellie wanted to let her know about Charlie Daniels. They would need to arrange a photo shoot with Joe as soon as possible, and she hoped they might even be able to make it for the following day.

As she went in through the main door, the first people she saw in the reception area were Sophie and Flynn. Sophie was carrying a huge bouquet of flowers, and Flynn had his arm around her. They looked blissfully happy.

"Ellie!"

"What gorgeous flowers!" said Ellie, admiring them hugely.

Sophie was beaming. "Aren't they?" She smiled at Flynn. "Flynn had them delivered. It was so romantic. And..." She looked questioningly at him. "We're definitely friends again, aren't we?"

Flynn leaned in and gave her a kiss. "And I promise not to interfere again. Or at least, I'll do my very best. Throw some wet clay at me if I do."

Everyone laughed.

"It's a promise," said Sophie.

Sophie turned to Ellie. "Don't worry about Angel. I gave Ferdinand to Debbie and she put him back in his basket. She texted me later to say that Angel didn't say a word."

"Phew!" Ellie felt very relieved. "What about the official at the Boat Show?"

"He was fine about it. He just told me not to flout rules in future, and saw me out. I gave him a little wave as I walked away."

Ellie giggled. "Trust you!"

"But what about you?" said Sophie. "Were the people on the boat helpful?"

"They certainly were!" said Ellie. "And now I must go and see Francesca. I hope she's still in the office."

"Okay," said Sophie. "Go on then. I must take these flowers home. See you tomorrow, Ellie."

"See you tomorrow."

In the lift on the way up to the office Ellie rehearsed what she would say to Francesca. She knew she'd love to appear cool about her success, but that probably she'd rush straight in and tell the Deputy Editor all about it. However, when she arrived in the office it seemed that Francesca already knew.

"Well," she greeted Ellie, "I've just had a call from Charlie Daniels's publicist. It seems you've got yourself an interview! Amazing!"

Piano was closing down her laptop, but her hands stopped moving, and hovered above the computer while she listened to Francesca.

"Angel wants to see you in her office right away. Congratulations, Ellie!"

"Thanks, Francesca!" Ellie smoothed down her hair and made her way towards Angel's office. Piano's face was a picture of mingled astonishment, fury and jealousy, but Ellie didn't care one bit.

"Come in, Ellie," said Angel, when Ellie knocked at the door. "Have a seat. Would you like a drink?"

The Editor in Chief had never treated her so

graciously and Ellie was shocked. She perched on the edge of one of the powder blue chairs and wondered about asking for a cup of tea. But she knew Piano would be asked to get it again and that Piano would hate her for it. Besides, it was the end of the day. She didn't need to be unkind to Piano.

"No thank you," she said.

"So. This interview," said Angel, all professional crispness. "We're told by Charlie Daniels's publicist that we can publish an article by you about the author in the next issue if we want. That's quite a scoop." She looked at Ellie. "In fact, with the Pop Lowther story as well, you've actually got us two scoops in one week. Is it your ambition to provide the entire content of our magazine in future?"

Ellie wasn't sure what to say. Was Angel pleased with her work, or not? It almost sounded as if she was angry. "Umm...well no... I'm sorry if..."

Angel raised one immaculately manicured finger to stop her. "That was a joke," she informed Ellie. "I am, of course, very pleased with you. If I have any complaint at all it's that I would wish for scoops to be more spaced out, instead of like buses, several arriving at the same time. Scoops sell magazines, but two at the same time don't sell twice as many copies." She paused, and smiled at Ellie. "However, I recognize that these things can't always be planned. Well done. Very well done indeed."

"Thank you," said Ellie, hoping that the Editor in Chief didn't intend to crack any more jokes.

Ellie got up to go, but as she reached the door Angel spoke again. "Ellie."

"Yes?"

"You had an almost impossible assignment and yet you pulled it off. I know there was a large element of luck involved, but that depended on you being alert and tenacious enough to take advantage of it when it came. It's not really my place to tell you this, but I believe your father would have been very proud of you. I'm certainly very pleased and proud to have you as a member of our team."

As Ellie made her way back to her desk Angel's words echoed in her mind. She could almost feel her father's presence, standing by her. And Ellie had never been more certain that this was the life for her.

For wannabe journalist, Ellie, doing work experience at her fave teen magazine is a dream come true. Check out the other titles in this stylish series:

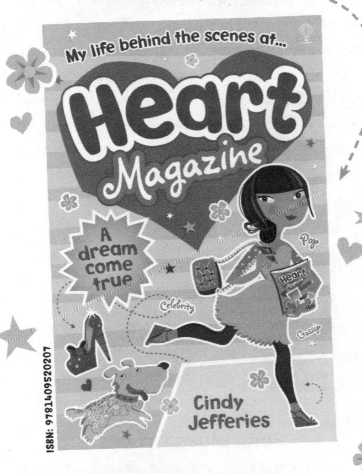

My life behind the scenes at...

Heart Magazine

A dream come true

Pop

Celebrity

Gossip

ISBN: 9781409520207

Cindy Jefferies

A dream come true

Ellie's got a jealous rival who's determined to turn her dream job into a nightmare...

Boys, blues & shoes

Ellie thinks she's going to miss out on meeting her
favourite band – until she finds herself on a photo
shoot with some very special 'extras'…

Best friends rock!

Ellie's fallen out with her best friend and an
interview with the son of a rock star is a disaster.
Will things ever go right this summer?

For more stylish reads
check out
www.fiction.usborne.com